# Lily Quench

## and the Dragon of Ashby

# Lily Quench

## and the Dragon of Ashby

## NATALIE JANE PRIOR

Illustrations by Janine Dawson

PUFFIN BOOKS

*For Felicity*

PUFFIN BOOKS
Published by Penguin Group
Penguin Young Readers Group,
345 Hudson Street, New York, New York 10014, U.S.A.
Penguin Books Ltd, 80 Strand, London WC2R ORL, England
Penguin Books Australia Ltd, 250 Camberwell Road, Camberwell, Victoria 3124, Australia
Penguin Books Canada Ltd, 10 Alcorn Avenue, Toronto, Ontario, Canada M4V 3B2
Penguin Books (N.Z.) Ltd, 182-190 Wairau Road, Auckland 10, New Zealand

First published in Australia and New Zealand by Hodder Headline Australia Pty Limited,
a member of the Hodder Headline Group, 1999
Published by Puffin Books, a division of Penguin Young Readers Group, 2004

7  9  10  8  6

Text copyright © Natalie Jane Prior, 1999
Illustrations copyright © Janine Dawson, 1999
All rights reserved

LIBRARY OF CONGRESS CATALOGING-IN-PUBLICATION DATA

Prior, Natalie Jane, 1963–
Lily Quench and the dragon of Ashby / Natalie Jane Prior ; illustrations by Janine Dawson.
p. cm.
Summary: Lily Quench, the last of a family of dragon slayers, befriends the dragon she is sent
to kill and together they join forces against an evil tyrant.
ISBN 978-0-14-240020-3
[1. Dragons—Fiction. 2. Friendship—Fiction. 3. Fantasy.]  I. Dawson, Janine, ill.  II. Title.
PZ7.P9373Lk2004  [Fic]—dc22  2003058432

Printed in the United States of America

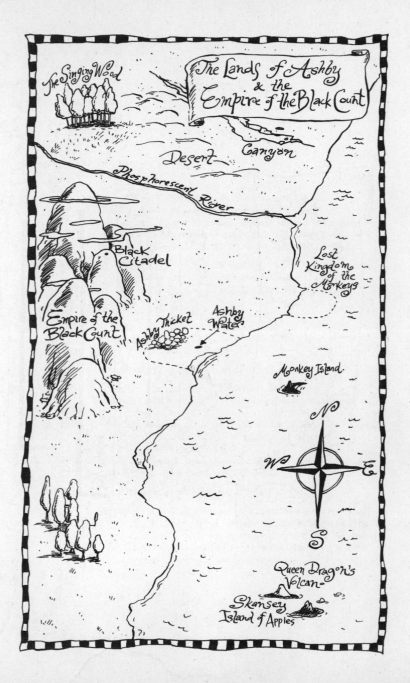

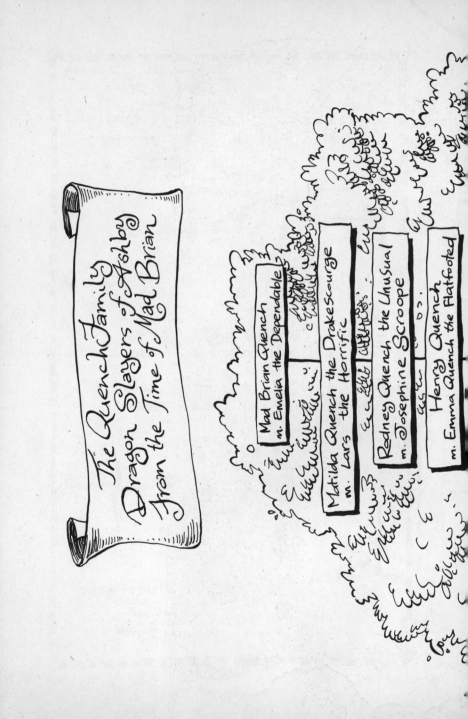

The Quench Family
Dragon Slayers of Ashby
From the Time of Mad Brian

Mad Brian Quench
m. Emelia the Dependable

Matilda Quench the DrakeScourge
m. Lars the Horrific

Rodney Quench the Unusual
m. Josephine Scroope

Henry Quench
m. Emma Quench the Flatfooted

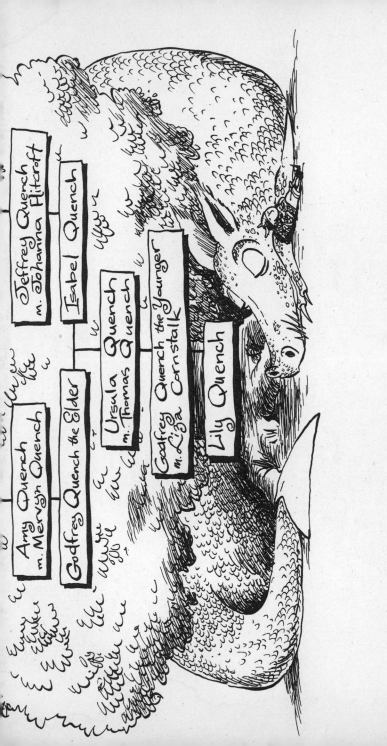

Jeffrey Quench m. Johanna Hitcroft

Isabel Quench

Amy Quench m. Mervyn Quench

Godfrey Quench the Elder

Ursula Quench m. Thomas Quench

Godfrey Quench the Younger m. Liza Cornstalk

Lily Quench

## chapter one
# The Coming of the Dragon

The dragon first appeared as a dot in the sky above Ashby Water, like a wisp of ash in the gray clouds of smoke hanging over the town. At first everyone was too busy working and minding their own business to notice it. But then the dot started circling, growing bigger and bigger until people stopped in the streets and pointed upward. The orphanage children marching around their exercise yard broke ranks and started yelling. Old ladies ran into their houses and shut the doors.

The dragon swooped over the Ashby grommet

factory, the dirty river and filthy streets, and the black church with the nailed-up door. Fire blasted from its nostrils, sending people running and screaming for their lives. It burned the jagged flag flying from the top of Ashby Castle and clipped the weathervane on the town hall with its wingtip. Then it settled on the scrap heap outside the grommet factory, breathing fire and beating its wings in a fiery crimson blur until the catches melted on the windows and the great iron factory gates glowed red hot.

In the castle where he ruled Ashby for the Black Count, Captain Zouche called an emergency meeting with his assistant, Miss Moldavia.

"This is totally unacceptable!" Zouche snarled as he paced the throne room. "The grommet factory has been forced to close for the first time since the Invasion! Send for the fire brigade. Send for the army. Send for whoever you have to, but I want that dragon dead!"

"I've done all those things already," said Miss Moldavia. "The fire brigade's been hosing the creature down since ten this morning. It doesn't seem to be making the slightest difference."

"What about the army?"

"Well, the tank unit broke down the factory gate, but was forced back by the heat. The artillery's bullets just bounce off its skin. If I were you," said Miss Moldavia, studying her perfectly painted fingernails, "I'd speak to whatshisname. You know. The librarian. This is a problem which requires planning, Zouchey. Research. Brains. All those things you're not awfully good at."

Captain Zouche scowled. He had been trying to get rid of the castle librarian for years.

"Do we have to?"

"Yes," said Miss Moldavia firmly. "As a matter of fact, I've already sent for him. That'll be him arriving now."

A soft tap sounded at the door. Miss Moldavia hopped off the mahogany table where she had been sitting and clicked across the room on high black heels. A tall young man with curly brown hair, forget-me-not blue eyes, and an anxious expression waited in the doorway. Captain Zouche caught one glimpse of the book he was carrying under his arm and looked as if he were about to throw up.

"Captain Zouche. Here is the librarian, er..."

"Lionel will do," said the librarian. He was used to people forgetting his name and had long since stopped minding when they did.

He placed the huge book reverently on the mahogany table and dusted off its leather binding. A picture of a dying dragon with a boar spear through its heart was stamped in gold on the front cover. The spear's shaft was broken and a five-pointed crown was hooked over it. Underneath was a motto in old-fashioned letters. Captain Zouche tried to read it, realized he couldn't, and pretended he hadn't even noticed it was there.

"Lionel," he said, "we have a problem. A problem with a dragon at the grommet factory. It has been suggested you might be able to help."

Lionel blinked. He thought of all the books he had pushed to the backs of the library shelves, and which he read secretly at night in his turret bedroom. Books about magic and faraway places, things no one had been allowed to talk about since the Black Count's Invasion. Shelved at 398.4

was a row of books about dragons. Lionel had read them all from cover to cover. In fact, it was safe to say he knew more about dragons than almost anybody else in Ashby.

"I think," he said, "what you need is a Quench."

Miss Moldavia sat up and started to look interested. The captain just looked annoyed.

"A quench? What do you mean, a quench?"

"Not a quench. A Quench." Lionel sounded a little firmer. "You see, sir, this isn't the first time Ashby's had this dragon problem. In the past, under the, ahem, kings' rule, they used to come nearly every summer. Queen Dragon. The Ashby Worm. Serpentine Bridgestock. There were lots of them. It's all written down here in the kings' chronicle." He tapped the book on the table. "This crown is the symbol of the kings and queens of Ashby. The spear and the dying dragon represent the Quenches. And here is the royal motto: **By Quenching We Rule**. Without the Quenches, there would have been no kings and queens. Without the Quenches, there would be no Ashby Water."

Captain Zouche made a growling noise. Miss Moldavia laid a warning hand on his arm.

"Go on, Lionel," she said. "Tell us what the book has to say."

"Well," said Lionel, flipping through the pages, "in the days when dragons were a problem, Ashby had its own family of dragon slayers. The Quenches. Here we have Mad Brian Quench, the first of the line. He rescued thirty-seven children from a dragon's lair in the mountains and returned them to their despairing parents. Then there was his daughter, Matilda Quench the Drakescourge. She killed two dragons with a single shot from her high-powered catapult. And Amy Quench and her twin brother Jeffrey—"

"Enough!" growled Captain Zouche. "That's quite enough. I'm not interested in listening to stories. Tell me, are there any of these... Quenches still left in Ashby?"

Lionel, who had just realized what was on the next page of the book, stopped flipping and went

very quiet. Miss Moldavia leaned forward and stabbed at a picture.

"Look at this!" she said. "It's a family tree of Quenches. Brian. Matilda...They're all here!" She ran her finger down the line. "They all seem to be marrying their cousins."

"That was to keep the dragon-slaying powers in the family," said Lionel. "It went against them in the end. The line dwindled away to almost nothing."

Miss Moldavia ignored him. "The last name is Ursula. Ursula Quench..."

"That old fright?" said the captain. "I've always thought she was mad. She lives next to the grommet factory, owes a fortune in back taxes. I was just about to throw her out of her house."

"Then it's as well you haven't," said Lionel. "If this book is right, Ursula Quench may be your only hope."

Something about the way he spoke made the others turn and look at him. Realizing he had gone too far, Lionel blinked and shrank away.

"Thank you, Lionel," said Miss Moldavia coldly. "You can go now. No, leave the book. It will be returned when and if we decide you may have it."

Together they watched him go, trailing down the long corridor from the throne room to the library turret. Captain Zouche waited until Lionel was out of sight, then kicked the door closed with his booted foot.

"Creep. We're going to have to get rid of him, Molly."

Miss Moldavia's eyes flickered over the portrait of the Black Count that hung over the battered throne. She picked up a copy of *Grommet News* that had fallen down behind the chair and tucked it under her arm.

"Yes," she said thoughtfully. "I rather think you're right."

## chapter two
# Lily Quench

While the dragon was settling into the grommet factory, the only person in Ashby who wasn't paying any attention to it was Lily Quench.

Lily had just buried her grandmother, old Ursula, in Ashby's small black cemetery. All through the burial rain had fallen, black with ash from the grommet factory smokestack. As she watched the grave·digger lower Ursula's coffin into the grave, Lily thought she heard screaming in the distance. But she had been too upset to really care.

Half of Lily was a Quench. Quenches did not cry under any circumstances. But Lily's mother had been Liza Cornstalk, senior gardener in the Ashby Botanic Gardens, and by the time she got home from the funeral, Lily's Cornstalk half had taken over. She let herself into the house, curled up in the parlor window seat with Ursula's cat-shaped cushion, and howled with sheer misery and desperation. In the morning, she would have to go and live in the orphanage and start work in the grommet factory. Grommeteers worked from dawn till dusk, in a dark sweaty factory. The closest they came to seeing the sun was the glow of red-hot metal discs dropping off the grommet production line. Everyone in Ashby knew that being a grommeteer was the most miserable fate on earth.

After a while, Lily's Quench half started to reassert itself. Her tears gave out, she hiccuped for a while, and then she sat up and blew her nose in her handkerchief. She was wringing out the drips when she happened to glance out the window and see a strange procession marching along the street.

First came a dozen soldiers in black uniforms—

a Black Squad from the count's army. They were followed by a smartly dressed woman with her hair swept up on top of her head, and a man everybody in Ashby Water would have recognized as Captain Zouche. At first, Lily assumed they must be going to the grommet factory, but to her amazement, when they reached her gate, the soldiers stepped back and allowed the woman and Captain Zouche to march down the path toward her door.

Lily jumped off the window seat. There was no knock, just a thud and a crash as the door was kicked in, and then the Black Squad burst into her tiny parlor.

"Ursula Quench," snapped the woman.

"No. I'm Lily. Lily Quench." As she looked at Miss Moldavia, the scaly patch on Lily's left elbow started to tingle and itch. Her back straightened, her chin went up, and something Quench-like swelled inside her.

Miss Moldavia looked down her nose and pursed her lips. "I mean, we want to speak to Ursula Quench."

"I'm sorry," said Lily. "My grandmother is dead." As she said these dreadful words, the unaccustomed feeling of bravery evaporated. Tears welled up in her eyes again and rolled down her cheeks. Captain Zouche went red and twitched alarmingly.

"Stop it!" he roared. "Stop it! If there's one thing I can't stand it's howling brats! Get rid of her, Molly! Men! I want Ursula Quench on this hearth rug within ten seconds, or I'll have this house torn down, brick by brick!"

"Captain, I really don't think that's possible," said Miss Moldavia. "The child just said her grandmother is dead. However, there is a chance we won't need her, anyway." She turned to Lily. "Did you say your name was Quench?"

Lily nodded.

"Granddaughter of Ursula, who was daughter of Isabel and Godfrey Quench the Elder? Five times great-granddaughter of Matilda Quench the Drakescourge?"

"I think so," said Lily doubtfully. Ursula had died before she could tell her much about their family history.

Miss Moldavia turned triumphantly to Captain Zouche. "You see, Captain? Indubitably, a Quench. Our dragon slayer is here."

"But I don't want to be a dragon slayer," said Lily.

"Want? Want?" screamed Captain Zouche, so loudly that both Lily and Miss Moldavia winced. "Who says you've got any choice in the matter? Let me remind you, girl, the Black Count rules here. If he says you'll slay dragons, slay dragons is exactly what you'll do."

"But I can't," protested Lily. "I don't know how. And besides, I haven't got anything to slay them with."

Captain Zouche looked like he was about to explode.

"Men!"

The Black Squad jumped to attention and unshouldered their rifles. Miss Moldavia's hand came down on Lily's shoulder like a vise, and then, at Captain Zouche's command, the soldiers started going through the house. They stabbed the chairs and beds with their bayonets and dumped out the cupboards and drawers; they ripped the curtains and the crocheted rugs Ursula had made during the winter; they threw Lily's precious books into the fire. Ursula's china tea set with the pink roses was smashed to smithereens in the fireplace, and the grandfather clock was stopped with one swift kick. Poor Lily did not know what to do. She

14

could only stand there, staring in horror at the destruction, while Miss Moldavia's sharp fingernails dug into her shoulder and stopped her from moving a single step.

At last, when the house was completely wrecked and almost everything in it was broken, the soldiers brought down a trunk they had found in the attic. The trunk was ancient and looked as if it had been burned, stabbed, and soaked at various times throughout its life; it was big enough for Lily to climb into and was sealed with a huge padlock. Attached to the handle was a label. Miss Moldavia untied it and read it out loud:

### DRAGON QUENCHING EQUIPMENT

"Excellent!" said Captain Zouche. He drew his pistol from his gun belt and blasted away the lock with a single shot. The lid flew open, and everyone crowded around.

Lily fell to her knees in front of the trunk. Old Ursula had possessed many peculiar treasures, but here were things Lily had never guessed existed. Inside the trunk, under a layer of old newspapers dating from the days of the Invasion of Ashby, was a photograph of Lily's father wearing a suit of armor. And underneath the photograph was a curious collection of objects, all jumbled together.

Captain Zouche took a bayonet from one of the soldiers and speared Lily's dead father through the heart.

"Creep," he said, removing the photograph from the bayonet's point with his boot. "I remember him, he was a filthy nuisance. What's that, Molly?"

"I think it's a list." Miss Moldavia pulled out a piece of paper and started to read. "'One fireproof cape—Brian Quench. One high-powered catapult —Matilda Drakescourge. One winged helmet, one bottle of Quenching Drops'—that'll be the crystal bottle with the dragon carving on it— 'two daggers (one silver with a dragon hilt), one collapsible boar spear, and one golden rope— Jeffrey Quench. One sword (broken), one shield (scorched), one suit of armor (incomplete).' The seven-league boots seem to be missing. Not that they're really needed, since the creature's practically next door."

As she spoke, a roar sounded from the grommet

factory. Someone screamed, a high, horrible, agonizing scream, and a sheet of red-and-purple flame shot past the window. Lily shuddered and clutched the bottle of Quenching Drops so tightly the dragon carving left an imprint on her hand.

Right now, a pair of seven-league boots would have been the best thing anyone could have given her.

Half an hour later, draped in Brian's cape and armed with Jeffrey Quench's rope, Quenching Drops, and boar spear, Lily found herself at the gate of the grommet factory.

The factory was built on the site of the old Ashby Botanic Gardens. Normally, endless clouds of black smoke streamed from its chimneys, and sometimes it was impossible to see where you were walking. But today there was no smoke: only billowing clouds of steam that poured out of the red-hot, buckled gates to the factory yard.

"What's all this water?" asked Lily, sloshing through puddles.

"The fire brigade," said Miss Moldavia. "They've been hosing the dragon down."

The temperature rose steadily around them. Lily felt sweat beads trickle down her forehead and saw Miss Moldavia dab her face with a lace-edged hankie. At the factory gates, the Black Squad soldiers fanned out behind her and raised their rifles. Lily saw there was no going back.

"Go on, girl. You're a Quench, aren't you? What are you waiting for?"

Lily straightened her shoulders. She took a step toward the gates and recoiled from the heat that blasted her in the face. Then she remembered the hood on her fireproof cape, pulled it up, and stepped through the gap.

Clouds of steam enveloped her. She could no longer see Captain Zouche, Miss Moldavia, or the soldiers; even the factory building was invisible. A pang of fear struck her heart, and then, as the vapor parted before her, she saw something gleaming on an enormous mountain of scrap metal.

It was dark red, the color of a peony, but it shone as if it were made of red-hot, burnished metal. Scales the size of dinner plates snaked down toward a flat-pointed barb that was so big Lily could have danced on it if she had been silly enough to try. It was the dragon's tail. The rest of the dragon was attached to it, but was so huge it was almost invisible in the swirling mists of steam that poured down from the top of the scrap heap.

Lily expanded her collapsible boar spear and walked as softly as she could around the heap. She saw the dragon's huge, clawed toenails, its flank like a crimson hill, and its front legs curled up as if in sleep. Quench-like, she climbed up the piles of metal rubbish until she stood in front of the dragon's head. Its eyes were closed, and several ugly teeth poked out of its mouth at uncomfortable angles. Black wisps of smoke floated from the creature's nostrils, but otherwise it was so still it might have been dead.

All she had to do was quench its fires and plunge her boar spear into its eye. Gently, Lily reached into her pocket for her Quenching Drops. She pulled out the crystal stopper and then, suddenly, without warning, her Cornstalk half took over.

A wave of unspeakable terror washed like a tidal wave over Lily's body. Her teeth rattled, her body shook, and as she tried to reseal the Quenching

Drops, her hand trembled so much the bottle slipped from her fingers and fell into the rubbish.

"No!" Appalled, Lily scrambled after it. The scrap heap shifted under her feet and the bottle rolled into a crack and disappeared. The dragon yawned, a huge, hot yawn that would have burned Lily to a crisp if she hadn't been wearing Brian's cape. Its tail twitched, and its eyelids opened. Two huge golden reptile eyes with black slits stared at Lily. She stared back, took a wobbly step sideways, and—

A piece of metal shifted under her feet, and the whole pile gave way, pitching Lily backward. She screamed, started to fall, and then, faster than she could blink, the dragon lunged forward and grabbed her in its mouth. Then, with a mighty kick from its hind legs, a smashing flick of its tail, and a swoop of its mighty wings, it sprang into the air and flew away.

## chapter three
## Queen Dragon

Inside the dragon's mouth, Lily screamed and tossed about. The tongue was scaly, hot, and wet, great gobs of slobber sloshed under her feet, and she could smell the metallic scent of molten grommets and old refrigerators. The dragon started to swallow and she felt herself sliding down a slippery red shaft to something as hot and horrible as the grommet factory blast furnace.

"He-e-e-elp!" At the last split second, Lily grabbed onto a dangly bit at the back of the throat. She stuck her boar spear into the tongue and catapulted forward like a pole-vaulter. The tongue moved convulsively as she grabbed the nearest tooth and lashed herself to it with Jeffrey Quench's golden rope. Then she wrapped Mad Brian's fireproof cape tightly around her shoulders and sat cross-legged on the dragon's scaly tongue. It wasn't comfortable, but at least it felt safer.

Lily peered out between the gaps in the dragon's teeth as if they were windows. They seemed to be flying mostly through clouds, but from time to time she caught glimpses of the sea rushing by below her. She could see ships as small as matchboxes, the occasional island, the spurts from a pod of whales. Finally, as the sun went down and night drew in, she could no longer see at all.

As Lily grew used to the idea of what was happening, flying became rather dull. She also began to feel drowsy. Partly, this was because the dragon's mouth was so warm; partly, it was because she was truly exhausted by all that had been happening. As soon as she convinced herself she was not in immediate danger of being swallowed, Lily curled up next to the dragon's tooth and started nodding off.

Dreams uncoiled like smoke inside her head:

dark dreams of Captain Zouche and Miss Moldavia, of people crying in the darkness, of a huge grommet that came down from the sky and held all of Ashby in an iron grip. Lily moaned and woke with a start. The dragon was starting to go down, not gently, but diving like an arrow from the sky.

Lily found herself slipping and sliding again. She screamed and clung to her rope, and as the dragon's mouth opened slightly she had a glimpse of waves, a cliff, and rocks bathed in moonlight. Then the dragon plunged into the sea, and everything was roaring darkness.

Lily floated back into consciousness on a cloud of steam.

At first she thought she was in a sauna, but then she realized she was lying on her back on a ledge of rock. She was still dressed in a rather damp fireproof cape, and beside her was a spear and a broken bit of rope that looked vaguely familiar. In the distance, someone was singing. Lily caught a whiff of sulfur; then the singing was interrupted by a loud burp and—

"Heavens!" said a voice. "It's alive!"

Lily screamed. She grabbed her spear and the golden rope and jumped behind the nearest rock. For as the mists cleared in front of her, she saw a crater filled with the most enormous pool of boiling mud. And bathing in it, with only its head and the tip of its tail protruding, was the dragon.

As Lily watched, the dragon started swimming toward her. Its tail sent waves of steaming mud rippling and splashing against the walls of the crater. Then it rose out of the mud pool. One huge front foot stepped onto the shingly beach below Lily's ledge, and then another. The dragon closed its eyes and shook itself clean like a dog. It lumbered forward until it was so close to the spot where Lily cowered that she could have stepped off onto the scaly space between its smoking nostrils.

Instead, Lily waved her spear like a pathetic toothpick and shrieked in a small high voice. "Stand back, dragon! Stand back or I'll kill you dead!"

To Lily's amazement, the dragon sat back on its haunches. "Kill me? Why would you do that?"

The answer leapt into Lily's mouth from nowhere. "Because I am a Quench, and killing dragons is what we do!"

"A Quench?" said the dragon incredulously. "You—a Quench?"

"Yes," said Lily. "Lily Quench." And because Ursula had taught her that it was wrong to make empty threats, she took careful aim with her spear, closed her eyes, and flung it at the dragon as hard as she could.

"Ow," said the dragon, and there was a clatter of metal on the rock. Lily opened her eyes and saw that her spear had hit the creature between the eyes and bounced off. "For a Quench, you don't have an awfully good aim. Besides, a boar spear is used for thrusting at close quarters. Not throwing. But I don't think you can be a Quench, really. When I think of that dreadful Brian with his endless piping, and Matilda with her BO and pimples—"

"She was my five times great-grandmother," said Lily coldly.

"Really? You poor child," said the dragon. "Well, I must say you don't look like her. Or any of the other Quenches I remember. For a start,

they all had the most awful scaly skin."

Lily looked at the dragon scornfully. She flicked back her cape, rolled back her sweater sleeve, and revealed the strange scaly patch on her left elbow. If the dragon could have gone white, it would have.

"Oh, dear," it said. "You are a Quench after all. How very depressing."

"Why?" said Lily, suddenly worried. "You're not going to eat me, are you?"

"Why would I do that?" said the dragon. "I'm afraid, my dear, you're extremely ignorant. Dragons don't eat people. They eat metal. What did you think I was doing on that scrap heap at the grommet factory?"

"I don't know."

"I was having breakfast. I'd been asleep for fifty years, and when I woke up I fancied a bit of iron. Of course, I could have eaten some of the gold I have in storage, but gold for a dragon is like chocolate for a human. Altogether too rich and sweet on an empty stomach."

Now, Lily had been born at the time of the Black Count's Invasion. Around this time practically every sort of interesting food had vanished from Ashby Water, so Lily had never tasted anything sweet except once, when Ursula's friend Lionel gave them some toffee. Lily had never forgotten the exquisite sensation of the sugar crackling on her tongue. So, although she had not really been following what the dragon was saying, and had never heard of chocolate, when she heard the word "sweet," something immediately clicked in her head.

"The Black Count won't let us have sweet things," she said. "It's against the public interest."

The dragon's eyes widened in astonishment. "Against the public interest? My dear child, why?"

Lily shrugged. "I don't know."

"I can tell you why," said the dragon. "Because if people ate sweets, they might actually enjoy themselves. Lily, why on earth are you working for these people?"

"I'm not working for them," said Lily, stung. "They *made* me help them. I didn't have any choice."

"Well, you do now," said the dragon. "Do you want to go back? If you do, I'll fly you straight back to Ashby Water."

"No!" exclaimed Lily. "No, don't do that! Please. I'd rather not."

"You see?" said the dragon. "You do have a choice after all. You know, Lily Quench, I've known a lot of dragons in my time. I'm ashamed to say, quite a few of them are not as well behaved as they should be. But I've never met one who's nearly as unpleasant as those people in Ashby."

For a long moment, Lily stared into the dragon's eyes. They were the clearest, most golden yellow she had ever seen, except for the pupil, which was blacker than the darkest night. Lily remembered the little she had ever heard about dragons: how they burned towns and ravaged the countryside, how they destroyed and devastated and devoured. This very dragon had done just that to the grommet factory—Lily had seen it with her own eyes. But Lily was also starting to think that the grommet factory was not such a loss, and that Miss Moldavia and Captain Zouche had behaved far more cruelly to the people of Ashby than this dragon ever could.

"Maybe," she said slowly, "Captain Zouche and Miss Moldavia are dragons in human skin."

"In that case, Lily Quench," said the dragon, folding its claws together and looking at Lily with an expression that reminded her unaccountably of old Ursula, "whose side are you on? The human dragons? Or the real one?"

Lily felt her elbow tingle. "I think...on the side of the real one," she said. "But who are you? And what's your name?"

"My name is Sinhault Fierdaze," said the dragon. "But most humans call me Queen Dragon."

# chapter four
# The Island of Apples

"And now, I suppose you're hungry," said Queen Dragon. "We'll have to find you some breakfast, but before we do, I think it would be a good idea to do something about your equipment. The Quenches have obviously fallen on hard times if those miserable bits and bobs are the best you could come up with."

"It was all I could carry," said Lily. "But I think I might know why there isn't much left. You see, during the Invasion, my grandmother and my father held Ashby Castle for King Alwyn. Then the Black Count sent his tanks to smash down the walls. My grandmother escaped, but the king and my father were killed. I think a lot of the equipment was lost in the final battle."

"What happened to your mother?" asked Queen Dragon. "Was she killed, too?"

"My mother was a Cornstalk," said Lily sadly. "She worked in the Botanic Gardens. After my father was killed and I was born, Captain Zouche ripped out the gardens and built the grommet factory. She died of a broken heart."

"How dreadful." Queen Dragon heaved a sigh. A huge tear glistened in her eye and plopped onto her nose, where it hissed and turned to steam. "It would never have happened in the days of the kings and queens."

"The kings and queens are gone," said Lily. "King Alwyn was killed and his son Prince Alwyn disappeared. No one has seen him since the Siege of Ashby."

"Well, that's encouraging," said Queen Dragon, perking up a little. "Just because no one's seen him doesn't mean he's gone for good. Maybe he's just missing . . . maybe he's even still alive! In fact, now you tell me this, a plan is starting to come to me.

But first things first. Armor, and then breakfast. Hop inside my mouth and I'll take you to my cave."

Lily supposed that if Queen Dragon had really wanted to eat her, she could have done so already. All the same, she couldn't help wishing she hadn't mentioned the word "breakfast." She climbed into the dragon's mouth and hung on to a tooth. Queen Dragon stood up and walked along the shingly beach toward a cave.

As soon as they entered the cave, everything went black. Lily started to panic, but Queen Dragon seemed to know where she was going. She walked along a passage for about a minute, then deposited Lily on the rocky floor.

"Now for some light." She snorted, and a ball of fire shot from one of her nostrils. There was a loud bang and, suddenly, a string of blue-and-yellow flames exploded into life around the enormous cavern.

"Oh!" cried Lily. "How beautiful!"

"Great, isn't it?" said Queen Dragon proudly. "My own idea. A personal gas-lighting system, fueled by vapors from the volcano. Some dragons would disagree, but I've always thought there's nothing worse than sitting in the dark."

But it was not the flare of gaslight that was holding Lily spellbound.

In the middle of the chamber, a mountain of gold crowns, coins, and armor stood as high as a four-story house. Chests of jewelry sparkled with precious stones, and diamonds and sapphires lay scattered over the floor. The treasure was more than a king's ransom: it was fifty kings' ransoms. As Lily stood, staring in amazement, Queen Dragon scooped up a golden clawful and popped it absently into her mouth.

"Excuse me," she said, crunching down on it. "I just fancied a snack. If you look over here, Lily, I think you'll find some suits of armor in your size."

She led the way around the hoard of treasure until they came to a smaller pile of discarded items. Chain mail shirts, plate armor, and helmets lay jumbled together, along with a selection of dresses, tunics, and other clothes. Lily's eyes fell on a green silk dress, embroidered with gold thread around the hem and cuffs. She picked it up and held it in front of her. It was the prettiest thing she had ever seen.

"You can have that, if you like," said Queen Dragon. "I think it came around a hundred years

ago with a chest of stuff from Tallowood Castle. Here, this mail shirt will probably fit you. The silver's been treated to ward off fire. That's why I've never eaten it, I suppose. Indigestible."

Something occurred to Lily.

"Queen Dragon," she said, "would you try and eat metal armor if it was on a person?"

The dragon blushed. "Well, I have eaten a few people by accident," she admitted. "They tasted awful, gave me heartburn. But don't worry. I won't swallow you if you're wearing treated armor. You'll need a sword and a helmet, too, Lily. What about that one over there with the little golden wings?"

Half an hour later, dressed in a silver mail shirt and winged helmet over her green silk dress, Lily emerged from the dragon's cavern. She had a new sword and shield, and a dagger in her belt, and she felt more like a Quench than she ever had in her life.

"We'll sit you on my head this time, I think," said Queen Dragon. She had obviously taken Lily's concerns about being eaten to heart. "There's a bony bit between my eyes; can you see it?"

"Yes." Lily clambered onto the dragon's head and made her way up her snout. She sat down on the scaly ridge and wrapped her arms around the bump. As a seat, it was surprisingly comfortable, and gave her a dragon's-eye view of everything around them.

"That's where we came in," said Queen Dragon, pointing to an opening in the crater's wall. "It goes out under the sea. We'll leave through the crater this time, I think. Hang on tight!" And before Lily had a chance to remember she had a drop of Cornstalk blood, the great red leathery wings swooped back and out, and they were airborne.

At first, all Lily could do was concentrate on holding on. It was a bit like the fastest, scariest fairground ride imaginable, though since Lily had grown up in Ashby Water, that wasn't saying very much. But after a minute or so had passed and she dared open her eyes, she realized that she was having tremendous fun. Unlike the journey the day before, she could see absolutely everything, from the clouds and birds to the wild rocky shores of the volcano poking up from the sea.

Here and there puffs of steam and yellow smoke shot out of cracks in the rock, and as they circled once and sailed away, Lily saw the waves breaking on a huge natural arch of rock.

Queen Dragon banked to one side and the volcano disappeared behind them. Ahead, a cluster of new islands sparkled like emeralds in the wrinkled sea.

"Is that where we're going?" Lily shouted, and Queen Dragon nodded, somehow catching the words above the sound of the wind rushing past.

She turned and headed for the largest island, swooping low over the others as she went. On one, Lily saw a few ruined huts and some sheep, but the others were only rocks and clumpy grass, and the smallest was just a spur of rock sticking out of the sea. Flocks of seabirds clamored and rose about them, and then Queen Dragon pulled in her wings and dived down to land on the largest island's grassy shore.

"Welcome to Skansey," she said as Lily climbed down. "I used to come here often. It's changed now, but if you look over there you'll see there's still plenty for you to eat. They call it the Island of Apples."

Because Lily had been born just after the Invasion, she didn't know what life in Ashby had been like before the count had come, but she knew from old Ursula's stories that things had once been different. The grommet factory hadn't existed; the river had been clear and sparkling; and every Sunday Ashby Church had been full of laughter and singing. In the castle, the kings and queens had ruled, for the most part, wisely and well. It was only when the Black Count had come that Ashby had turned into the gray, dismal place that was all Lily knew.

So as she sat in the orchard with the dragon, munching apples until the juice ran down her chin onto her mail shirt, her Quench half began to wonder—just wonder—whether Queen Dragon was right, and it might be possible to do something about it. But her Cornstalk half wasn't certain, so she pushed the thought to the back of her mind and left it there.

"What is this place?" she asked.

"It used to be a farm," said Queen Dragon. "A man lived here many years ago; his name was

41

Daniel. He planted the orchard and farmed the
sheep. I suppose you could have called him my
friend."

"What happened to him?"

"He grew old and died," said Queen Dragon
sadly. "That's the problem with humans—you live
such a little time. All of a sudden his hair grew
white, and then one day he just wasn't there
anymore. The house started falling down, and the
orchard became overgrown. I haven't been to this
island in over sixty years."

"I like it here," said Lily. She wiped her hands
on the grass and leaned back against the tree. "I'd
like to live somewhere like this."

"Maybe you will one day," said Queen Dragon.
"But first, we have work to do. It seems to me
that what we need to do is find Prince Alwyn.
Of course, he may be dead. But if he's alive, he
is the rightful king."

"He wasn't much older than I am now when
the count invaded," said Lily. "If he escaped, he'd
be grown up now."

"In my experience, people rarely disappear
completely," said Queen Dragon. She looked
around at the trees and the sheep grazing in the

orchard. "I've been giving this some thought, and it seems to me the best thing you can do for Ashby is find out whether the prince is alive or dead. And the best way of doing that is to head for the Cave of Secrets. It's an oracle, hidden deep in the Singing Wood. Or at least it used to be there, unless your friend the Black Count has chopped the wood down."

"He's not my friend," retorted Lily. "What's an oracle?"

"An oracle is a place where you can learn what will happen in the future," Queen Dragon explained. "The Pool in the Cave of Secrets is one of the most powerful oracles there is. Every visitor can ask one question. The Oracle will always give a truthful answer, but in return the visitor has to give up whatever means most to them in all the world. If we ask where Prince Alwyn is, the Pool will tell us."

Lily shivered. Even though the sun was shining, a dark cloud seemed suddenly to have passed over the island. She tried to think of what she wanted most in all the world, but all she could see were the cores of the apples she had eaten, turning brown on the rich, green grass.

## chapter five
# Dragon's Flight

While Lily gathered some apples to eat on the journey, Queen Dragon took off and did some reconnaissance. She gauged the directions of the winds and measured their strength, and sniffed the air for any hint of approaching storms. The flight to the Cave of Secrets would be a long one, and there were few places for them to rest along the way.

"I'm getting old," Queen Dragon explained when she came back, "and I'm not as tough as I used to be. In fact, I can't remember the last time

I visited the Singing Wood. It must be centuries."

"How old are you?" asked Lily as they readied for takeoff.

"Oh, about three thousand years or so," said Queen Dragon carelessly. "I've forgotten exactly. Dragons don't worry about birthdays much. We have too many of them."

They took off, and Lily watched the Island of Apples with its sheep and ruined huts disappear behind them. She was rather sorry to see it go. The sight of the daisies and other wildflowers waving in the breeze made her itch to get down and start growing things. In Ashby, when she had tried to plant things in the garden, the smoke from the grommet factory killed everything as soon as it was planted. Bulbs, trees, flowers—Lily would go out in the morning and find them shriveled in the beds, and none of the seeds she planted even came up. Old Ursula had never understood why she found this so upsetting, but Lily knew it was something she had inherited from her mother. Maybe, if things changed and Prince Alwyn returned, the Ashby Botanic Gardens would be filled with flowers again. But for the moment, the grommet factory ruled.

In the castle throne room in Ashby Water, a meeting was taking place. The lights were dim, for night had fallen, and all available power had been redirected to the factory. Outside, it was raining, and an occasional flash of lightning sent an eerie shimmer across the mahogany tabletop.

The Black Count's portrait looked down from above the throne with a sinister eye. Miss Moldavia paced the room, her hands clasped behind her back.

"The grommet stockpile is down by thirty percent, ladies and gentlemen," she said. "Not only that, since the dragon's visit production has slumped to an all-time low. This morning we received a letter from the Black Citadel, from the count himself, advising us of his dissatisfaction. If the factory's output is not back to full capacity by the end of the week, he has instructed us to relieve all of you of your positions as directors."

"And you all know what that means!" snarled Captain Zouche.

The three directors paled.

"Yes. All ex-directors will take their place with

the grommeteers on the factory production line," said Miss Moldavia. "I suggest, ladies and gentlemen, it would be wise to give some thought to how you might stop any future dragon attacks. Now that Lily Quench is gone, it might not be so easy to get rid of the dragon next time."

"Are there no other Quenches left?" asked a middle-aged woman with sharp-looking teeth.

"We believe not, Crystal."

"And a good thing, too," quavered an old man. "There's enough talk among the grommeteers as it is."

"Talk? What talk?" barked Captain Zouche. "Nobody in the factory's allowed to talk. It's a rule."

Crystal gave a nervous laugh. "I'm afraid, Captain, it's a difficult rule to enforce. You see, no matter what we do, the grommeteers see each other out of hours. They all live in the same buildings. They eat in the same canteens. So they chat to each other. They have nothing else to amuse them."

"They are obviously not working long enough hours, then," said Miss Moldavia. "If I were you,

Crystal, I would put them all on double shifts until this crisis is resolved. May I ask what sort of talk there is between them?"

Crystal looked rather sick. "Well...I'm not really sure. To be honest, I don't have that much to do with them."

"I can tell you," said a voice from the other end of the table.

Lightning struck, and there was a rumble of thunder. Everyone swiveled their chairs around to see who had spoken. Miss Moldavia folded her arms.

"Evangeline? Perhaps you might like to share your knowledge?"

The youngest director stood up and cleared her throat. She was slim and dark-eyed, with a pretty face and a glossy black sweep of hair across her forehead. But her face was thickly made up, and her mouth had a downward turn that made her look dissatisfied and grumpy.

"There's talk in the factory about the Old Days," she said. "That's what the grommeteers call the time before the Invasion. Of course, the older ones remember it. They say that one day Prince Alwyn will come back and Ashby will have a king again."

The room went deathly silent. At last, very quietly, Miss Moldavia spoke.

"How did you learn this, Evangeline?"

Evangeline blushed. Under heavy makeup and purple rouge the effect was not attractive. Across the table, Crystal shook her head disgustedly. She was Evangeline's mother, though usually she pretended she was only her sister.

"I know," Crystal said. "She's slumming it down in the backstreets with her disgusting friends. They dress up as grommeteers and go and hang out at the factory bars."

"It's all right, though," said the old man, Harold. He was Evangeline's grandfather. "Without a Quench to crown him, Prince Alwyn can never become king." As if he realized he had said too much, he suddenly went silent. The room was still. Miss Moldavia could have heard a pin drop.

"I see," she said. "Maybe we had better have a proper explanation of this... Quench business as soon as possible. In the meantime, I suggest we split the factory shifts. Crystal, I want all the old grommeteers together, and I want them working double time. Evangeline, keep your ear to the ground. If anyone is caught telling stories about the Old Days, send them to me. And now I think we'll call this meeting to a close."

The directors and Captain Zouche gathered up their things and left. Only Miss Moldavia remained. For a long time she stood staring at the picture of the count above the throne while lightning flashed and the rain pattered endlessly on the castle roof. Then she picked up her papers, switched out the light, and silently left the room.

The sun was going down and the stars were starting to come out over the Southern Ocean. Flying across the sea, Lily and Queen Dragon had made fair progress since leaving the Island of Apples, and were starting to think about stopping for the night.

"There's an island up ahead," said Lily, pointing. "Maybe we should stay there."

"An island?" Queen Dragon peered through a drift of cloud that floated below them and tried to identify where they were. "Hmm. I haven't been there in centuries. As I recall, it used to be uninhabited. But there's fresh water and a nice sandy beach, so it will do for the night. Hold on, Lily. Going in."

Clouds brushed wetly against Lily's face as they descended, and a moment later they emerged beneath the cloud cover into clear air. Ahead, she could see the island quite clearly. Its boomerang shape was dark against the water; there was a bay on the protected side, and it was covered with tall trees. But although it was too dark to see much else, there could be no doubt about the lights that twinkled along the shoreline and on the waters of the bay.

"Queen Dragon! I don't think the island's uninhabited anymore!" Lily gasped. But just as the words left her mouth, there was a whiz, a thud, and a soft cry from the dragon. Her wings faltered in midstroke; she lurched and tried to recover. Then her eyes rolled back in her head and she started to fall out of the sky.

"Queen Dragon! Queen Dragon, what's happening!" Lily shrieked, but Queen Dragon was unconscious or dead, and made no reply. Out of control, she spiraled down toward the waiting lights, a wickedly barbed arrow protruding from

between two scales. The force of the air rushing past her ripped Lily from the dragon's back. With a shrill scream she flipped backward, head over heels, then plunged like a star into the sea.

## chapter six
# Monkey Island

Lily sank down through the water, stunned by her fall and barely conscious of what was happening. Her silver armor weighed her down, carrying her to the bottom of the sea. As she breathed in choking, burning lungfuls of water, she realized she was going to die and that there was absolutely nothing she could do to stop it.

Then she heard something plunge into the water from far above. A second splash followed the first, and Lily realized two rescuers were swimming powerfully toward her. Strong hands grabbed her arms, and, together, her rescuers started swimming back to the surface, pulling her behind .hem.

Lily's head burst through the surface of the sea. More hands reached down and hauled her out of the water onto a raft and she lolled helplessly, vomiting water as her rescuers chattered around her in shrill, high voices. A short distance away, the enormous form of Queen Dragon floated unconscious on the water of the bay, surrounded by rafts that swarmed with small brown figures.

"Welcome to Monkey Island," said a voice. "Here's hoping you've got a good reason for being here." An ugly, clever-looking face loomed above her. Lily screamed, and fainted.

In her office in Ashby Castle, Miss Moldavia laid aside the reports from the grommet factory and turned to the young woman who was seated across from her.

"Let me get this straight, Evangeline," she said. "Your grandfather says that unless the king of Ashby is crowned by a Quench, he can never be the true monarch. Is that right?"

Evangeline sat uncomfortably on the edge of the black leather chair and nodded.

"And that furthermore," pursued Miss Moldavia, "Prince Alwyn, son of King Alwyn the Last, did not die in the Siege of Ashby Castle, but escaped. You're certain this is what your grandfather believes?"

"Well, that's what he told me, ma'am," said Evangeline. "You've got to understand, Grandpa is very old. Sometimes he gets things wrong. But he was quite definite that King—Prince— Alwyn escaped the Siege. Grandpa was locked up in the castle prison. He saw Prince Alwyn and a woman leave through a secret tunnel somewhere in the dungeons. He thinks," Evangeline added, "that the woman was someone called Ursula Quench."

"Hmm," said Miss Moldavia. "Yet he said nothing about it at the time. Why?"

Evangeline shrugged. "No one asked him. Everyone assumed the prince was dead; I think Grandpa just forgot. But now there are all these rumors, he's remembered. Ever since the meeting he hasn't been able to talk about anything else."

"I wonder," said Miss Moldavia, "who started the rumors off in the first place." She sat and brooded for a moment. "Evangeline, thank you for telling me this. You've been very helpful. Of course, since all the Quenches are dead, we have nothing to fear. If Prince Alwyn turns up, he cannot be crowned. But I think it would be prudent if we could lay these rumors to rest.

"This is what I would like you to do. Go to the library and talk to the librarian. Tell him what your grandfather told you about Prince Alwyn's escape and see what the castle records have to say. Find out what he can tell you about this secret passage—if it's still there, and whether he's got a map showing where it is. And see if you can get to the bottom of this story about the Quenches crowning the king. Report as soon as you have news." Miss Moldavia paused. "Oh. And Evangeline...I don't think there's any reason to speak to Captain Zouche about any of this. He's a busy man. We don't want to trouble him."

"No, ma'am." Evangeline stood up and bowed politely. "I'll report back to you as quickly as I can."

Monkey Island was neither large nor particularly remarkable. It had one beautiful, horseshoe-shaped bay, into which Queen Dragon had fallen, a single town, and lots of rain forest. From the hill, which was the highest point above the sea, it was possible to see the entire island, and for this reason, a permanent lookout tower had been established there. When Lily's captor carried her up the hill, trussed like a chicken and barely conscious, a watchmonkey came running down and demanded to know their business.

"Corporal Max with a human prisoner, to see His Majesty."

The watchmonkey saluted and waved them on. Lily was carried across a bridge into a nearby building. Slung as she was over the monkey's shoulders, it was hard to see much, but the building seemed to be made of timber and woven palm fronds suspended around a clump of enormous palm trees. Monkeys were everywhere, bustling along the corridors and running up and down the trees to various upper levels. Small monkeys worked in gangs sweeping the floors,

and larger monkeys carried things around, while several chimpanzees in suits of flashy yellow velvet wandered up and down and oversaw the others. Their chatter was deafening, and it was all incredibly filthy. The smell of unwashed monkey, old bananas, and rotten mango was so strong that Lily felt as if she were going to faint all over again.

At the end of the corridor, another guard stopped them and asked their business. Corporal Max bowed, explained once again, and waited while the guard went into a nearby room. A minute or so passed, and then he returned and ushered them inside. The room was large, stuffy, and lit with dozens of tiny banana oil lamps that made it smell even ranker than the corridor.

"Corporal Max with a human prisoner, to see His Majesty," announced the guard, and Lily was dumped unceremoniously on the floor.

"Release the human," said a clear high voice.

Corporal Max took a knife out of his pocket and sawed through her bonds. Lily winced. A pair of crimson slippers stuck out from under a nearby desk, and as she lifted her eyes she saw in astonishment that the person who was wearing them was another monkey, enormously fat, and dressed in a blue silk dressing gown and feathered hat.

"Bow, girl. Bow!" hissed Corporal Max.

Lily staggered to her feet and bowed as humbly as she could. The monkey king—for such he was—looked her over a moment longer.

"What is your name, human?"

"Lily Quench, Your Majesty."

"Lily Quench?" The king's eyes narrowed. "From Ashby Water?"

"Y-e-es." All at once, Lily started wondering whether she had said the right thing. But the king did not press her any further. Instead he clapped his hands. Corporal Max immediately left the room. Lily and the monkey king were alone.

"Sit down, girl," he said, and Lily pulled up a rickety cane chair. She was glad to sit, for her head was aching and she felt giddy from being carried upside down. Mosquitoes buzzed, and the scent of the oil lamps tickled her nostrils.

The monkey king sorted some papers and put them away in a drawer. Then he hopped up from his chair, opened a cupboard, and took out a bowl of freshly ripened mangoes.

"Miss Quench. Will you join me?"

"Thank you." Lily helped herself to a mango and peeled away the skin from the flesh. Juice squirted all over her armor as well as on the monkey king's desk, but fortunately he didn't seem to mind. While she gnawed her way through the sticky fruit, he ate three, skin and all, leaving nothing but the pit, which he tossed on the floor.

"I must apologize for the way you've been treated, Miss Quench," he said, pulling a string of mango from between his teeth. "Of course, if we had known who you were, we would have been more careful. Corporal Max can be over-enthusiastic, and your dragon gave him a fright."

Suddenly, Lily remembered Queen Dragon, floating unconscious on the water of the bay. "Queen Dragon! Is she all right?"

"Quite all right," the monkey king assured her. "It was just a sleep dart. She'll already be recovering."

"May I see her?" asked Lily.

"As soon as she is awake, my servants will let us know," said the king. "So tell me, Miss Quench, what brings you to Monkey Island? And how is my old friend, King Alwyn, and his family?"

"King Alwyn is dead," said Lily. "His son, the prince, is lost. Queen Dragon and I are on our way to the Pool of the Oracle to try and find him."

"Indeed?" The king looked interested.

"Yes." Lily nodded. "Things in Ashby are very bad." She told the king all about the Black Count, Captain Zouche and the grommet factory, and her quest to change things. When she had finished, the monkey king shook his head.

"Shocking," he said. "Miss Quench, you have my sympathy. We must talk about how Monkey Island can help you. But first, I think it would be a good idea if you rested. Corporal Max will come and show you to a suite."

The king reached for a bell on the other side of his desk and rang it. As he leaned forward, a chain and medal fell out of the open neck of his blue silk gown. It was not a very attractive piece of jewelry, but something about it caught Lily's eye. Suddenly, she realized why, and froze.

The chain was made of Ashby grommets linked together. And the medal was a profile portrait of the Black Count.

Lily looked at the king, and the king looked at her. Their eyes locked, and, for a moment, neither of them seemed to know what to do. Then the monkey king lunged at her. His fat stomach crashed into the desk and his fingers grazed her throat, but Lily was thinner than he was and her reflexes were just a bit quicker. With a bound, she kicked over her chair and ran for the door.

The king rang his bell furiously. "Guards! Guards!" he shrieked. Lily reached the door, but it was too late. She could already hear running feet in the corridor. Corporal Max and a band of monkeys were on their way, and she knew she would never be able to outrun them. Suddenly, a roar sounded in the darkness outside, and she looked up in wild hope. A huge Quench-like wave passed over her, and she knew what she had to do.

While the monkey king screamed and jumped up and down, Lily grabbed the nearest tier of oil lamps and sent it crashing over. Flaming banana oil shot across the floor, and the woven palm fronds burst into flame, forcing Corporal Max and his followers back. Lily ran to the window and threw open the shutters. Below her, a crowd of terrified shrieking monkeys surged up the hillside. Sure enough, a huge dark shape was soaring overhead.

"Queen Dragon!" Lily cried at the top of her voice, and the dragon, hearing, pulled in her wings and swooped in as if for the kill. Lily climbed up on the windowsill, felt the flames at her back as the building caught fire, and jumped. The night air whistled through her hair, the ground rushed up—and then Queen Dragon snatched her up in her mouth and they were gone.

From the top of the nearby watchtower where he had taken refuge, the monkey king watched Lily and Queen Dragon disappear into the clouds. Below him, his palace burned fiercely, the dried palm frond walls falling in on themselves and sending sparks into the night. The king ground his teeth. Then he turned to his secretary, a sweet young thing in a snappy skirt and red high-heeled shoes, and told her to get out her notebook.

"Take down a letter, Ariel," he said brusquely. "Address it to Captain Zouche at Ashby Water, from his affectionate friend, Montague Rex."

For the next few minutes, the king dictated a letter, then got Ariel to read it back to him. When she finished, he sealed it with his medal, and nodded. "That will do," he said. "Arrange a courier bird—I want it sent tonight. Lily Quench and her dragon friend might have escaped us, but they won't get away with this."

As he spoke, the roof of his palace collapsed with a roar of flame. The monkey king turned away, wrapped his dressing gown tightly around him, and stood, staring broodingly into the night.

## chapter seven
# Evangeline

Evangeline sat on her penthouse roof, with her makeup off and her bare feet propped up on the railing. In her left hand she held a cherry cocktail, which she was sipping delicately through a straw. Loud music blared from a radio at her elbow, but though from time to time she wiggled her toes, she wasn't really listening to it. Instead she stared at the orange glare of the grommet factory, silhouetted against the night sky, and thought about Miss Moldavia.

Evangeline's family, the Brights, was one of the

richest and most powerful in Ashby Water. Once, though, her grandfather Harold had been a thief, and her mother, Crystal, had made a living ripping off old ladies by selling them false insurance policies. No one in Ashby wanted anything to do with them. So, when the Black Count's army invaded and Captain Zouche found Harold in prison, it had been natural for her grandfather to offer his services to the invaders.

Ever since then, the Brights had prospered. Evangeline had a fast sports car, a posh apartment, and a place on the board of the grommet factory when she felt like doing some work. But in spite of this, she was not a happy person. And though she couldn't explain why at night she sat on the roof of her penthouse, looking at the clouds of smoke and the red sparks flying from the chimneys of the grommet factory, and wished— just wished—she could see the stars, sometimes these feelings became so strong they frightened her. Then Evangeline would drive off at top speed in her sports car and look for a new boyfriend, or dress up as a grommeteer and hang out in the backstreets with her friends. But this sort of thing kept her mind off things only for a little while, and meanwhile, underneath, some rebellious, deep-seated dissatisfaction grew like a flower from a seed and sent down roots.

Unlike most people in Ashby, Evangeline was in a position to know that it was Miss Moldavia who told Captain Zouche—and everyone—what to do. So, after a while, when she had finished her drink and it was getting too cold to sit outside, she went into her bedroom and dressed herself in a leather top and trousers and a pair of boots with six-inch heels. Then she put on her makeup, teetered down to the garage, and drove off at top speed into the night.

"That was a close call," said Queen Dragon as she and Lily flew away from Monkey Island. "Just as well it was only a sleeping dart—and that the monkeys were too stupid to tie me up properly. I don't think they realized I would snap out of it quite so rapidly. But I could have sworn that island was uninhabited last time I flew over it."

"I suppose it could have been," said Lily. "Maybe

the monkeys have only lived there a little while."

"There was talk once of a kingdom of monkeys on the mainland," Queen Dragon mused. "They lived on an isolated peninsula, cut off from the rest of the world. Then around a hundred years ago, there was an earthquake and a huge tidal wave, and the whole peninsula disappeared into the sea. I wonder if these monkeys are related?"

"Maybe," said Lily. "But they're certainly not cut off." She told Queen Dragon about the medal around the monkey king's neck, and how she had accidentally told him the details of their quest.

"Hmm. That's bad news," said Queen Dragon, when Lily had finished the story. "The last thing we want is Captain Zouche getting wind of what we're planning. There's nothing else to do, Lily: we must get to the Singing Wood as quickly as possible. At least the winds are with us. I should be strong enough to fly there without stopping."

She lifted her head and rose upward through the clouds. Lily sat on her perch, listening to the wind rushing past, and wondered about the Oracle and the Cave of Secrets. It was all rather scary. Suppose she got the question wrong, and couldn't ask another? And what about the sacrifice she had to make to get the answer? Lily wasn't sure what it was she wanted more than anything else in the world, but if it was that important, she was certain she wouldn't want to give it up.

They flew on for a day and a night, crossing the coast just before sunset, and passing over strange and, for the most part, uninhabited country. Lily slept in snatches, waking in time for the moonrise, and again when Queen Dragon roused her to see a great phosphorescent river, flowing through a desert far below. It was desolate and rather frightening, like a stream of molten silver lighting up the night, and when they veered away from it and flew along a canyon instead, a cloud of giant bats rose out of a cavern and flew along with them. Once, a bat swooped so close its wing grazed Lily's cheek and she screamed and nearly fell off. But then Queen Dragon, who did not seem to mind the creatures the way Lily did, snorted a fireball into the night and sent them chittering and flapping off to a safe distance; and when they reached the end of the canyon and started flying over the desert again, the bats wheeled about and flew off, heading back to their camp in the rocks to wait out the day.

Dawn came, a thin ring of golden fire around the eastern horizon, and with it, Queen Dragon banked and started flying to the north. Around this time, Lily became aware of a change in the scenery. The desert, which had seemed never-ending, began to give way to rocky, scrubby country and then plains of grass dotted with smooth-trunked trees. The wind whispered and wove strange patterns through the grass. Ahead, a purplish haze resolved into a gray-green band of vegetation.

"The Singing Wood," said Queen Dragon, and she started flying lower. The wood was enormous, disappearing toward the horizon, and Lily, who had never seen so many trees in her life, began to feel dismayed. How on earth would they find the Pool of the Oracle in there? She supposed they might fly over the top of it, but the trees were so thick there would be nowhere to land. Sure enough, as they approached the Singing Wood, Queen Dragon folded back her wings and glided steadily downward, coming in for a perfect landing just at the edge of the trees.

She dropped her head and Lily scrambled down

into the grass. It was soft and pale green, contrasting oddly with Queen Dragon's huge crimson flanks, and was almost as tall as Lily. But there was nobody anywhere about to see them, though insects buzzed in the grass, and a few birds sang sweetly as they darted across the cloudless sky.

Lily stretched her stiffened arms and legs and started walking toward the Singing Wood. It was strange, she thought, the way the grassland suddenly stopped and the wood began. Then, all of a sudden, she walked—*bang!*—into something invisible. It was as if an unseen barrier had been erected between her and the trees.

"The Singing Wood is a special place, Lily," said Queen Dragon. "You can't just wander in. In fact, without a good reason for visiting, we'd never even have found it."

"What do we do?" asked Lily.

"We wait for a Guide," said Queen Dragon, and with that she curled herself up and fell asleep.

Evangeline parked her car outside Ashby Castle and flashed her director's pass to the guard on duty. The library was in the South Turret. Evangeline stalked across the courtyard, past several Black Squads doing drills for Captain Zouche, and entered a small wooden door at the foot of the tower.

The South Turret was the oldest part of Ashby Castle and had been badly damaged in the Siege. Here, Godfrey Quench the Younger and King Alwyn the Last had fought their final battle, and since Captain Zouche did not like to be reminded of them, he had never bothered to repair it. As Evangeline climbed the stairs she could see bullet holes in the walls and black scorch marks where the tower had burned. Finally, she reached the third floor where the library was and laid her hand on its enormous iron knocker. Then she paused, listened, and took away her hand. Somebody inside was reading out loud.

It was the story of Queen Elspeth the Magnificent, Mad Brian Quench, and the Lost Children of Ashby. Lionel had read the story many times before, and because he knew it so well he was able to use different voices for all the characters and put in lots of expression. But Evangeline had never heard it, partly because it was one of the books that Lionel kept hidden at the back of the shelves, and partly because she had never heard anybody read any story before in her life. So, instead of going inside and asking him about Prince Alwyn and the Quenches as Miss Moldavia had told her to, she sat down on the stone floor outside the door and listened as intently as if she were under a spell.

At last the chapter came to an end. The story's magic slowly faded and Evangeline heard the reader sigh and put aside the book. At once she felt an enormous rush of disappointment. The reading was over, and the moment was gone; she would never find out what happened next. Evangeline could not bear the thought. She jumped to her feet and, without even pausing to bang on the knocker, threw open the door and stumbled inside.

The room was old and shabby. It was badly lit from a single high window, and full of sagging shelves stacked with ancient books. Rolled-up maps spilled out of pigeonholes and bundles of yellow newspapers wobbled in stacks around the room's circular walls. A card catalog teetered on three legs, propped up by an atlas, and in the midst of all this confusion one person, a young man, sat at a desk. Evangeline saw that he had curly brown hair and clear blue eyes the color of forget-me-nots. On the desk in front of him was a large book called *DDC21 Vol. 2* and another one called *Grommet Production Techniques: A Manual.* When he saw Evangeline, he hastily picked up a pencil.

"Who are you?" he demanded. "What are you doing here? The library is closed." He sounded angry and alarmed, but Evangeline was past caring what he thought of her behavior.

"I'm Evangeline Bright," she blurted out. "Please. Don't stop reading. I want to find out what happens next."

Miss Moldavia sat at her dressing table, looking disconsolately into her mirror. She did not like what she saw. Once, she had been beautiful, with long silky brown hair, skin like milk, and green eyes her admirers compared to chips of jade. Now her hair was dyed black, her skin was plastered with makeup, and the slanted green eyes had lines at the corners no face-lift could get rid of. Years of politics, scheming, and too many cherry cocktails at bedtime had eaten away at her loveliness, until her bloom had withered and fallen. She was getting old. And, like most people who use beauty as a weapon, she was aware that the power it gave her was on the wane.

Miss Moldavia reached for her cocktail, started

to sip it, and then thought better and put it aside. The scars from her last face-lift had scarcely faded, and she could already see new wrinkles forming. No! There had to be a better way. Miss Moldavia looked around her room and her eyes fell on a thick, red book that had somehow made its way to the pile on her bedside table. Unlike Captain Zouche, Miss Moldavia was a great reader, and though she could not remember where the red book had come from, something about it—she could not say precisely what—struck a chord in her memory.

Miss Moldavia got up, lifted aside the latest issue of *Torture Weekly,* and retrieved the book. A dying dragon stared up at her from the cover, and she realized it was the copy of the kings' chronicle she had taken from Lionel, the librarian. Captain Zouche would have tossed it into the bin without a second thought, but Miss Moldavia was cleverer than that. She took the book back to her dressing table and started flipping through it. The book was filled with the history of Ashby, starting with Queen Elspeth the Magnificent and continuing to the reign of the last king, Alwyn the Ninth. Interspersed with the deeds of the kings and queens were stories about the Quench family, and on page 289, Miss Moldavia finally found what she was looking for: the Quench family tree. Miss Moldavia studied it carefully, then turned the page and, unexpectedly, found a second chart.

Miss Moldavia sat up. For a moment, she stared at a name on the bottom of the page, and her eyes narrowed as she thought things through. Then she reached for her cocktail, popped the maraschino cherry absentmindedly into her mouth, and, settling back in her chair, began to read.

## chapter eight
# The Cave of Secrets

Lily was very tired. The sun was high and beat down uncomfortably on the grasslands at the edge of the Singing Wood; she could not sleep and was hungry and thirsty. There was not so much as a tree to shade her from the heat, and she could feel sweat prickling across her forehead. So, while Queen Dragon slept, Lily decided she would walk along the edge of the wood. Everything was so lush and green, she was sure there must be a river or at least a stream she could drink from. If she was lucky, there might even be some berries on a bush.

Lily scrambled to her feet and walked up to the spot where the invisible barrier had stopped her. She took a careful step or two forward, holding her hand out in front of her, and then, to her surprise, realized that the barrier had disappeared and that the way into the Singing Wood was open. Growing increasingly excited, she started to walk quickly until the sun stopped beating down on her head and she found herself among trees.

Lily turned and saw that the wood had closed behind her. Vines trailed down from the gnarled branches of the trees, and there was moss on the trunks. In the distance, she could hear the sound of a stream gurgling over rocks, but there was no path to point the way. If she kept walking, in another minute she would be lost. Too late, Lily remembered what Queen Dragon had

said about waiting for a Guide.

And then she saw a figure coming toward her through the trees: a sturdy, gray-haired woman in a blue dress. Lily stood staring at her. Shock seeped through her body and she felt faint, unable to trust her eyes. It was a dream, it had to be, or else . . . The woman reached a clearing in the trees. She stopped, smiled, held out her arms, and Lily broke into a run.

"Granny!" In another moment Lily had flung herself into Ursula's arms. Then her grandmother's own arms were around her, and she realized that this was no dream, no illusion, no mistake.

Ursula was real—and alive.

"But you're dead!" gasped Lily, when she had recovered enough from her shock to say something. "Granny, what are you doing here? How can you be alive?" She thought of something horrible. "You're not a ghost, are you?"

Ursula laughed, her own deep, throaty laugh that made Lily's heart feel glad.

"Of course not. There's no such thing as ghosts. Haven't I told you that? And no," Ursula went on, "before you ask me, you're not dead either. Believe me, child, you're as alive as you ever were, and I am more alive than I ever was. That is the great benefit of being dead. The only disadvantage is that once you've died, you can't come back to the world you've left—except to a few special places. As soon as I saw you heading for the Singing Wood, I came to meet you.

"Your mother and father send their love and best wishes for your quest. We know all about it. And I can tell you one thing already. Prince Alwyn is still alive. I helped rescue him from the Siege, and the Pool in the Cave of Secrets will show you where to find him."

She took Lily by the hand and together they started walking through the trees. Much to Lily's surprise, a path magically appeared where there had been none before, wending its way between trees and into clearings where the sun's rays broke briefly through the canopy. From time to time they emerged into larger clearings where wooden houses had been built and gardens planted. Wisps of smoke floated from the chimneys and in some of the gardens people stood, hoeing up weeds, or planting vegetables, or chatting. When she passed each group, they smiled at her, and waved and called, "Good luck, Lily!"

"How do those people know who I am?" asked Lily.

"The Oracle has told them," explained Ursula. "They are the forest Guides, descendants of people who have come here over the years to consult the Oracle. Sometimes, the journey to the

Singing Wood is so long and hard the questers cannot bear the thought of going back. So they stay here and make homes, and act as Guides when people come from the outside world."

"You mean, people live here?" Lily stared at some children playing in a garden, and an idea began forming in her head. "Granny... when my quest is over and we've found Prince Alwyn, could I come back here? I could build a house and grow vegetables, and you could come and see me whenever you liked."

"You could, indeed," agreed Ursula. "I would like that very much. But first, you must speak with the Oracle. And since it is a long walk, it occurs to me that it might be a good idea for you to have something to eat. The last house is just coming up."

They stopped at a picket gate and a woman came out and asked if she could help the visitor to the Oracle. Lily asked for a cup of water, which was immediately brought for her, along with a piping hot potato cake and a bowl of raspberries and cream. The water was fresh and cold, and as she ate Lily realized she had forgotten how hungry she was. She was not tired anymore, either. The Singing Wood seemed to have that effect on people.

Ursula sat with her, and when she had finished they thanked the woman for her hospitality and went on their way.

"And now," said Ursula, "we are on our own until we reach the Oracle. You can see the ground is starting to rise. The Cave of Secrets is on the edge of a mountain range. To reach it we must cross the Deepest Chasm."

"The Deepest Chasm?" echoed Lily. "What's that?"

"You'll see for yourself in a moment," said Ursula, and they climbed over the crest of a hill and came down into a valley. Lily gasped. A huge jagged crack opened up in the earth, as wide as a broad river and stretching in either direction as far as they could see.

The sun was not quite overhead, and though Lily could see a long way down before the chasm faded into shadow and darkness, the bottom was invisible. A waterfall poured over the cliff on the opposite side and disappeared, as if it were draining into endless nothingness. All at once, Lily's Quench-like courage evaporated. She said nothing, but followed Ursula down the path to a tiny thatched hut, nestled on a spur of rock jutting out over the chasm.

Inside the hut, several wicker baskets, each one just big enough to hold a single person, were lined up against one wall, and a complicated system of ropes and pulleys stretched through an opening, out across the gorge. Ursula took a basket and hooked it onto the rope.

"Hop in."

Lily stared at her beseechingly. "Is it safe?"

"Of course it's safe," said Ursula. "The Guides keep it maintained. You have no choice, Lily, if you want to reach the Oracle. There is no other way to cross the chasm. Climb in, and the basket will take you across."

Reluctantly, Lily climbed into the tiny basket. Ursula waited until she was settled, then reached for a lever on the wall. The basket skidded and bounced across the floor. Lily shrieked, closed her eyes, and then swung out wildly over the chasm.

The sensation was terrifying—much worse than flying on a dragon's head. The basket was fragile and swung giddily on its hook, and when she peeked, Lily could see the horrible nothingness of the chasm through the wicker. She huddled down as low as she could, and then gradually, as the basket stopped swaying, she realized it was not so bad. The other side was already coming up, and when she glanced back over her shoulder, she could see Ursula waving from a basket of her own.

Almost before she realized the trip was over, the basket reached the cliff on the other side of the chasm. Lily jumped out, breathlessly. A moment later Ursula arrived beside her.

"We're nearly there, Lily," she said. "The Cave of Secrets is just around the corner. See, here is the path." She pulled aside a branch and revealed a tiny path, like a fairy track, disappearing through the undergrowth.

They followed the path through the bushes for several minutes, until they heard the sound of another waterfall. Then the path came out into a clearing. A large pool, surrounded by trees, filled most of it, and it was into this pool that the waterfall poured. Behind the waterfall, a low arch of rock led into what Lily guessed must be the Cave of Secrets.

"The Oracle knows you are here, Lily," said

Ursula solemnly. "It knows everyone who comes to speak with it. All you have to do is swim under the waterfall and through the arch. When you reach the Cave of Secrets, you must lie down beside the Pool of the Oracle and whisper what you want to know. Ask one question only, and the Oracle will answer truthfully. But make sure it is the right question, for if you waste it, you may not ask another."

Lily bit her lip. "Come with me, Granny," she begged. "It will be easier if you're there to help."

Ursula shook her head. "I can't, Lily. Only the living can visit the Pool of the Oracle, and only one person may enter the Cave of Secrets at a time. Otherwise it is no longer a secret. You must go alone."

Lily drew a deep breath. "All right."

Shivering, she pulled off her dress and armor until she was wearing only her petticoat. She felt cold and exposed, and dreaded what she would find on the other side of the rocky archway. But there was nothing for it but to go. Lily dipped one toe into the water, and then her foot. It was ice-cold and perfectly clear and pure.

Leaving Ursula watching from the poolside, Lily

started to wade into the water. The cold bit at her flesh, creeping up her body until it reached her waist, her chest, her neck. Suddenly, the rocks disappeared under her feet and she could no longer stand up. Keeping her head above water, Lily kicked out and started paddling toward the waterfall.

The giant trees cast shadows over her, and ahead she could see the waterfall, huge and deadly. The closer she got to it, the more terrified she felt. All Lily could think of was her fall from Queen Dragon's back on Monkey Island; how the water had filled her lungs, and how she had nearly drowned in the sea. Now the waterfall's spume speckled her face, and she could feel the current created by its fall drawing her in. Lily drew one last deep breath, said a silent, frantic prayer—and dived.

The waters of the pool closed over her head. Lily could not see anything, but the weight of the water bore her down. She struck out, kicking madly through the mighty swirl of the waterfall's downfall, and then, suddenly, the waterfall was behind her. Ahead, a dark archway of rock opened up. Lily swam toward it. Her lungs were already almost bursting, and the tunnel was longer than she had expected; she didn't think she was going to make it . . . Then light showed, her head broke through the water, and there was silence and blessed rock under her feet.

She was in the Cave of Secrets. And it was the most beautiful place she had ever seen in her life.

The Cave of Secrets was almost, but not quite, circular. Its rock walls were irregular, and here and there some velvet moss and a few ferns grew in the rocky crevices. Light slanted in from a hole in the roof and illuminated the cave, picking up flecks of pure gold in the rock and sending an emerald gleam sparkling over the surface of the small, clear Pool at the cavern's heart.

Lily walked out of the waterfall pool and crossed the rocky floor of the cave. There was something magical about the quietness here, for she could not hear the waterfall, or even the sound of birdsong, only the bubble of a small spring of water feeding quietly up to fill the Pool. In front of her was a bare platform of rock, just big enough for her to lie on.

Lily lay down on the rock and her cold body magically stopped shivering. She leaned forward and whispered her question to the Oracle.

"Pool of the Oracle, where can I find Prince Alwyn?"

Her whisper fluttered around the cave and faded away. Lily waited. Then, so softly she almost did not hear it, the Pool whispered back the answer. An image floated in the water, and she leaned forward, straining to catch it before it disappeared, the moment stretching into an eternity. Suddenly, Lily realized that time here ran very thin, that the Oracle was in the past, present, and future all at once, and that this was why the Singing Wood was the only place where the living and the dead could meet. If she wanted to, she could pass a hundred years here in the blink of an eye, could live a thousand lifetimes, or die forever and never be forgotten.

Time stretched out. She saw her face in the water of the Pool, growing older and wiser and more beautiful, and herself dressed in silver armor, standing in a garden with a dark red rose in her hand. Then the images started crowding in on her, so many, so bright, and so varied that Lily could no longer keep up with them.

Her face touched the water. She cried out, the spell broke, and she was alone.

## chapter nine
# The Net Tightens

Lily swam back under the waterfall and emerged in the outer pool. Ursula was waiting for her, sitting cross-legged on the rock. When Lily climbed out, she helped her off with her petticoat and pulled her dry dress over her head. "Are you all right?"

"Nnnn—" said Lily, her teeth chattering. "C-cold." She squeezed water out of her hair and stamped her blue feet on the rock. Ursula put an arm around her and hugged her.

"Well done, Lily," she said. "I'm proud of you.

Now put on your boots and I'll take you back."

Lily took Ursula's hand and together they retraced their steps. As they went, Lily's spirits gradually lifted. She thought about what the Oracle had told her, and somehow everything made sense. In fact, now that she knew Prince Alwyn was alive and where she could find him, it was even becoming a little exciting. In her mind's eye she saw herself single-handedly defeating Captain Zouche and turning back the Black Squads to Ashby's farthest borders. Then, she and Queen Dragon would fly back to the Singing Wood, and she and Ursula would live happily ever after.

After a while, the trees began to thin, and she could see the grassland beyond the forest. At the edge of the trees, Ursula turned to Lily and took her hands.

"Lily. You are about to embark on a dangerous mission. I wish I could go with you, but I can't, so instead I will tell you a secret. There is a passage leading into Ashby Castle, the same one I helped Prince Alwyn escape through during the Invasion. The outside entrance is in the crypt under Ashby Church. You must go there and look for the tombs of the Quenches. When you find Matilda Drakescourge's tomb, search for the word 'Quench' on the left-hand side. Push the letter Q upward and the entrance to the tunnel will open in the floor.

"There is something else you must know, too. Lily, the kings of Ashby can only be crowned by a Quench of the true line of Brian and Matilda. When you have defeated the enemy and restored Prince Alwyn to his throne, you must be there at the coronation to place the crown on his head. Promise me, Lily. You are the only Quench left; if you're not there to crown Prince Alwyn, Ashby Water will be in the hands of the Black Count forever."

"I promise," said Lily.

"Good girl," said Ursula, and she squeezed Lily's hands. "And now, it is time to say good-bye. Let me look at you one last time and give you a kiss. We will not see each other again."

"N-not meet again?" Lily stammered. "But I thought I was coming back!"

Ursula shook her head. "Child, you have forgotten the Oracle. The price for the question you have asked is to give up the thing that means most to you in all the world. The Singing Wood is closed to you forever. You may never return."

Lily burst into tears. She flung her arms around Ursula, and Ursula held her tightly. Then the wood began to sing. Every tree, every rock, every stream keened a beautiful dirge, and above them Lily heard the voices of the forest dwellers, lifted in lamentation. Slowly, the song and the wood began to fade around her. First the trees, and then the rocks and streams, started disappearing, and finally Ursula herself stepped back and lifted her hand in farewell. Then she, too, was gone. The song faded into silence, and Lily fell forward into the sighing grass and wept.

About the same time Lily and Ursula were saying good-bye, three important things were happening in Ashby Water.

First, a weary courier pigeon from Monkey Island flapped its way into the Ashby Castle dovecote. It was the bird King Montague of Monkey Island had sent after Lily's escape. The guard in charge of the dovecote untied the message capsule from the pigeon's leg, put the bird in a cage, and took the letter to Captain Zouche.

The second important thing was this: as luck would have it, when the letter arrived, Captain Zouche was with Miss Moldavia.

The captain took one look at Miss Ariel's splodgy typing and handed it to his assistant. "Here, Molly. You read it."

Miss Moldavia unrolled the tiny scroll and read the letter out in a slow, dispassionate voice. It told how Lily Quench was still alive, how she and her dragon accomplice had escaped from Monkey Island, and how they were planning to restore Prince Alwyn to the throne of Ashby. Even before she finished reading, Captain Zouche started throwing a tantrum that lasted for the best part of half an hour.

"So Lily Quench is still alive," said Miss Moldavia when he had finished. She did not seem very upset herself. "Don't worry, Zouchey. It's one thing for Lily Quench to have escaped an island full of monkeys, but quite another for her to get away from us."

"Creep!" fumed Captain Zouche. "Creep!"

"Oh, come on, Zouchey," said Miss Moldavia impatiently. "Do you really think Lily Quench will find Prince Alwyn before we do? Even assuming he's still alive? Tell you what: if it upsets you so much, why don't you put me in charge of it? I'll give the matter my full attention and find out exactly what's what."

"All right, Molly," said Captain Zouche, little realizing that his agreeing was the third important thing. "You take over. And whatever else you do, make sure you deal with Lily Quench."

Miss Moldavia smiled a secret smile. "I will, Zouchey," she promised him. "I will."

Mr. Hartley was the minister of Ashby Church, but because the church had been boarded up when the Black Count invaded, this was not saying very much. The count hated singing, hated people being happy, and took a dim view of God as someone who got in his way. The law said there were to be no more hymns, no more weddings, and no more church services in Ashby. Fortunately, Mr. Hartley took a different view.

Ever since the Invasion, Mr. Hartley had worked on in secret. He held services in deserted warehouses, performed marriages in cellars, and crept into sick people's homes to pray with them. Though once or twice a Black Squad had come close, by the time they tracked him down and smashed their way in, Mr. Hartley had always vanished. But brave and resourceful as he was, he had always known that one day he would be caught.

So, when Mr. Hartley was woken by the sound of a door being kicked in and heavy boots clattering up the stairs to the attic where he was hiding, he was not surprised. He threw off his blanket, grabbed his escape bag, and ran for the window, which he had left unlocked. (He always slept in his clothes, so there was no need to change.) But as he started scrambling out onto the roof, his sleeve caught on the window catch. The moment he paused to untangle himself was all his enemies needed.

With a *bang!* the attic door flew open and he was hauled, yelling and kicking, back into the room. The Black Squad gagged him, tied him up, and marched him off in the direction of Ashby Castle. Here Mr. Hartley was dragged down a slimy set of stairs into the dungeons and chained to the wall. No food or drink was given to him, and there was no light to see by. Mr. Hartley shivered with cold and tried not to think about the rats squeaking and rustling in the darkness.

Time passed. Mr. Hartley did not know how long, but he grew hungrier and thirstier and more afraid. His arms ached agonizingly in their sockets as he hung from the wall.

At last, a light appeared in the corridor, shining this way and that as if somebody was trying to find their way. A key scraped in the lock, and the gate of his cell screeched open.

The yellow beam of a flashlight passed over the floor and swung up across his body until it reached his face. Mr. Hartley blinked painfully and screwed up his eyes.

"Who are you? What do you want with me?" he rasped.

A woman laughed unpleasantly. "I want to speak to you about a wedding."

Meanwhile, upstairs in the turret, Evangeline and Lionel were lying on the library carpet, reading.

It was a cold night and a small fire was burning in the hearth. Evangeline was making toast on a fork and spreading it with raspberry jam she had brought with her from her apartment. A pot of tea was brewing on a trivet. Just as the toast was done and the tea was ready to be poured, Lionel reached the end of the chapter and closed the book.

"Delicious." He bit into the toast Evangeline handed him and gazed contentedly around the room. For the first time in years, he had someone to share his books with. Every evening since her unexpected arrival in the library, Lionel and Evangeline had met in secret to read the books he had hidden at the back of the shelves; she had even borrowed some to read by herself. Stories of the Quenches and the kings and queens of Ashby Water, books about dragons and magical happenings in faraway places. They were also starting to tell each other their own, made-up stories. Evangeline's were wild and full of improbable adventures and people, while Lionel's were often sad, though he would not say why.

Lionel speared another piece of bread on the toasting fork and held it out toward the fire. Suddenly his eyes widened. Was it his imagination or was there a dragon flying toward them through the flames? Lionel blinked, and the dragon was gone. He looked at Evangeline and realized from the expression on her face that she had seen it, too.

"Evangeline—" Lionel began, but the next words never reached his lips. With a noise like a thunderclap, the door and window of the library exploded inward.

As if from nowhere, a Black Squad appeared, sliding down ropes, leaping in through the window, and streaming in through the broken door. Evangeline and Lionel screamed and grabbed at each other. The teapot flew off its stand and smashed on the floor, and the book Lionel had been reading fell against the grate and started to smolder.

"What's happening?" yelled Evangeline. "What are you doing? Stop!" For the Black Squad was overturning the library shelves, kicking aside books and newspapers, and stabbing with their bayonets at the maps and paintings. Evangeline jumped up and lunged at the nearest soldier with her toasting fork. Lionel grabbed her hand and wrenched her away.

"Let me go!"

"No! Leave it!" Lionel dragged her across the room, dodging soldiers and crawling over broken tables and capsized shelves. "Come with me, quickly!"

Behind the librarian's desk was a tiny door. Lionel jerked down the handle, and it opened onto a stairway, winding up and down the turret where he slept. He pulled Evangeline in after him and slammed the door. Skittering on her high heels, Evangeline panicked and started running up the stairs.

"No!" cried Lionel. "Not upstairs! Down. Down!"

He yanked her back in the other direction. But it was too late. A second Black Squad was already marching up the stairs.

Evangeline screamed once, and then the squad engulfed them. Fighting and kicking, they were lifted off their feet and carried back up to the library, where they were thrown, sprawling in a heap on the floor. The fire was out and every shelf had been demolished. Maps had been pulled to pieces and the floor was strewn with the torn and broken pages of books.

Lionel looked at the devastation, lowered his eyes, and was silent. Beside him, Evangeline was crying. It was the first time she had cried since she was a little girl, and she almost felt surprised she was able to do it. Even odder, she found she was crying mostly for Lionel. Until this evening, Evangeline had never felt anything for anyone else in her whole life. Then Miss Moldavia stepped through the ruined door and walked toward her, and she could only feel terror for herself.

"Evangeline. I'm disappointed in you. I thought you showed promise, and you have let me down."

"No!" Evangeline began to protest, but a soldier had already grabbed her and dragged her to her feet. Miss Moldavia nodded her head toward the broken door.

"I don't think so, Evangeline. In fact, since you seem so attached to the grommeteers, I think you should join them. There's a night shift starting at the factory at ten o'clock. Corporal, tell the supervisor I want this woman down at the blast furnace, shoveling coal."

"What!" cried Evangeline. "No! You can't do this to me! You can't!"

"I can, I'm afraid," said Miss Moldavia. She watched as Evangeline was dragged screaming down the corridor, and then turned to Lionel, who was being held by four burly soldiers.

"And now, Mr. Librarian," said Miss Moldavia, "we have things to discuss. This masquerade has gone on for too long."

"I agree," said Lionel unexpectedly. Despite the soldiers who surrounded him, his expression when he looked at her was hard and terrible. It was as if something had happened to tear away the mask that covered his face and reveal a different person who had always lurked underneath. Many people might have quailed before the look on Lionel's face. Many more might have gone down on their knees. But Miss Moldavia, though outwardly human, was inwardly made of cast iron, like a grommet.

"Take him to the dungeons," she said curtly. "Chain him up with that traitor, Hartley. We'll soon see if he's as brave as he makes out." Then she swung around on her spiked black heels and swept out of the room.

## chapter ten
# The Secret Passage

Shortly before midnight, after a journey of several days, Queen Dragon came down to a field outside of Ashby Thicket. The lights of the town twinkled in the distance, and there was an orange glow from the grommet factory. It was cold and the dragon's feet and tail sent sizzling puffs of steam up from the damp grass. As soon as they had reached the cover of the trees, Lily slid down the dragon's snout and flexed her aching muscles.

"This is as close to Ashby as I dare come,"

Queen Dragon said. "That's the main road over there; you'll have to walk into town alone. Pity we didn't think to bring along a cape of invisibility."

"I didn't think there was such a thing," remarked Lily.

"You'd be amazed at the things people come up with when they want to kill a dragon," said Queen Dragon darkly. "Now, Lily, have I got this right? You go into Ashby, find the secret passage, and enter the castle. At dawn, I attack the town from the air and distract Captain Zouche, Miss Moldavia, and the Black Squads. Meanwhile, you find Prince Alwyn and call on the grommeteers to witness his coronation. Then everyone turns and drives the Black Count's followers out of Ashby."

"I think that's right," said Lily. When they had worked it out, the plan had seemed a good one, but listening to it again, she wasn't so sure. She felt especially nervous about setting out on her own. Though she knew it wasn't practical for a dragon the size of a house to sneak into Ashby Castle, she would still have felt a lot safer if Queen Dragon could have been there.

"Brave heart, Lily," said Queen Dragon.

"Remember: you're a Quench."

"A Quench who feels like a Cornstalk," said Lily. She pulled off her mail shirt and helmet so she wouldn't draw attention to herself, and tucked them under a bush. Then, picking up her long green skirts, she started walking into town.

It was a clear night, and the moon cast a pale bluish light across her path. For the first few miles, Ashby River gurgled alongside the road, and because it was late there was hardly any traffic—only the occasional truck carrying grommets, and some rich young friends of Evangeline's who roared past once in a sleek red sports car. Lily hid in the bushes by the side of the road when they approached, and waited until they were gone. But slowly, as she got closer to Ashby, the landscape began to change: the river wound its way into the sludge-choked Ashby Canal, the trees and shrubs gave way to yards and warehouses, and smoke from the grommet factory filled the skies and blotted out the stars.

Lily kept to the backstreets and walked with her head tucked down. From time to time she passed a grommeteer on his way to the night shift, or a dirty child out on his own and up to no good. But no one stopped her, and at length she came out of the shadows into the blackened forecourt of Ashby Church.

Why had Captain Zouche never knocked it down? Lily did not know. She only knew that the church had been boarded up soon after she was born, and that until tonight she had never been inside it. Feeling more like a Cornstalk than ever, she crept up the blackened steps and pushed her dagger into the gap between the first board and the door. The rotted wood splintered and gave way with a frightful crack. Lily peered through a splintered panel and punched a bigger hole in it with her dagger hilt. She put her hand through the gap and lifted the latch on the other side.

The door creaked loudly when she put her shoulder to it, and lurched off one of its hinges. Lily quickly squeezed inside and wedged it shut. She took a stub of candle from her pocket, lit it with a match, and looked around the sad and desolate place.

Dust and spiderwebs hung from the broken light fittings, pulpit, and altar. The stained-glass windows were smashed and boarded over, and pigeons nested in the intricately carved woodwork overhead. Lily picked her way around piles of pigeon dung, her feet leaving a trail in the dust that covered the floor. At the foot of the bell tower, she found a trapdoor and a huge iron ring sticking up from the floor.

Lily grabbed the ring and heaved. At first, it seemed as if the trapdoor was stuck, but then the hinges groaned and it shifted unexpectedly. A gust of cool air rose up. Lily leaned the trapdoor back against the wall and peered into the hole at her feet.

A spiral staircase wound down into the bowels of the church. Lily took a step down, and then another, keeping her right hand against the wall as she felt her way. At the foot of the staircase she found another door, locked, and a giant key hanging on a hook on the opposite wall. It turned easily when Lily put it into the keyhole, and the door opened onto a long, stone, vaulted room. It was the church crypt—the burial place of the Quench family since the days of Brian and Matilda.

It looked ancient, Lily thought, far older than the church that stood above it. Stone tombs were dotted around the room, and the walls were covered with plaques remembering the people who were buried under the floor. All the

Quenches were here, except for Ursula, who was buried in the cemetery. Lily walked around, reading the inscriptions. Here were the twins, Amy and Jeffrey of the golden rope; beautiful Isabel, who had crowned King Edgar the Miserable; even Lily's father, Godfrey the Younger, whose simple plaque gave only his name. The oldest graves of all were the stone chests. Lily found Mad Brian, and then, at the very end of the room, the tomb she was looking for:

HIC JACET

&

MATILDA QUENCH
DRAKESCOURGE

BY QUENCHING WE RULE

A statue of Matilda lay on top of the tomb, carved in stone. She was wearing a long dress and armor, with a sword at her side. Despite what Queen Dragon had said, there was no sign at all of any pimples on her face. If anything, she looked a bit like Ursula. Lily, who had always been a little frightened of Matilda Drakescourge, immediately felt better. She found the word "Quench" on the left side of the tomb and pushed the Q firmly upward.

At once there was a grating noise underfoot, as if some ancient winch had been set to work beneath the floor. Slowly, a massive panel of stone dropped away and swung out of sight. Lily gripped her candle and looked anxiously into the narrow crawl space it had revealed. Then, with one last backward glance, she hitched up her skirts and disappeared into the secret tunnel.

Lionel sat, manacled, on the edge of a hard wooden bench in the castle dungeon. Beside him was Mr. Hartley, his hands chained to the wall. On a chair opposite them both sat Miss Moldavia. She was red with anger. The prisoners were pale and exhausted.

"You obviously don't realize, Prince Alwyn," said Miss Moldavia, "that if I wanted to, I could have you tortured. Very subtly, very painfully, so it wouldn't show. You should be grateful that I shrink from injuring my future husband."

"Don't call me Alwyn," said the librarian wearily. "I've already told you, I haven't been called that since I was a little boy. And I'm not your future husband."

"Your name is Alwyn. Crown Prince Alwyn Lionel Perceval of Ashby," repeated Miss Moldavia. "I saw it on the family tree in that ridiculous chronicle of yours, and I'll thank you to stop pretending."

"If you've read the chronicle," said Lionel, "you should know that marrying me is pointless. No king of Ashby can be crowned except by a Quench. Without one, it doesn't matter what my name is, and who my parents were. You might as well save yourself the trouble and let me go."

"Let you go? So you can tell Zouche what I've been up to? I hardly think so," said Miss Moldavia tartly. She turned to Mr. Hartley. "I understand you hate rats, Mr. Hartley. Would you rethink your stand on performing the marriage if I put you in a cell full of the creatures? Imagine them crawling over your face and body, nibbling at your feet, and wriggling up your trouser legs. I can easily arrange for it, if you continue to be stubborn."

Mr. Hartley shook his head. "Never. I will never marry you to a man who is not willing."

"In that case," said Miss Moldavia, losing patience, "we will have to see what we can do about getting his consent." She went over to the gate of the cell to where the torturer was waiting. "Mr. Trench? Take the new prisoner into one of the interrogation rooms. I wish to speak to him alone." She waited while Lionel was unchained and led away from the cell, then added to Mr. Hartley, "We'll deal with you shortly."

The gate clanged shut. Mr. Hartley shuddered and slumped back against the wall. He was cold and hungry, and his arms were numb from being chained; but nothing—nothing—was so bad as the thought of the rats. Yet what could he do? If he married Miss Moldavia to Lionel, he would only help make her queen of Ashby. Mr. Hartley closed his eyes and prayed. Suddenly a creaking noise sounded in the corner; he started on his bench and then—

"Ssh!" said a voice, and a tiny light appeared, floating toward him through the darkness. It was being carried by a fair-haired angel in a green silk dress, and Mr. Hartley almost fainted with shock. Then the angel's face came into focus, and he realized he knew who it was.

"Lily Quench!" he exclaimed. "What are you doing here?"

"I've come to help you," said Lily. "There's a secret passage from here to the church. Did you know that?"

"Never," said Mr. Hartley. Then he remembered something. "Lily, you must be careful! Miss Moldavia has Prince Alwyn captive. She is trying to force me to marry her to him. If she finds you here, she'll make you crown him king of Ashby. Then she will be queen, and there'll be no stopping her!"

Lily went pale. "Lionel is being held captive?"

Mr. Hartley nodded. "Miss Moldavia's taken him to an interrogation room."

"Then I must find out what has happened to him." Lily climbed up onto the bench and tried to force open Mr. Hartley's manacles with her dagger. "It's no good—the locks are too strong. Do you know where the key is?"

"Miss Moldavia has it," said Mr. Hartley. "Lily, leave it. Prince Alwyn is more important. Ashby is more important. Go now, and see what you can do to help!"

Lily hesitated a moment, then jumped off the bench onto the floor. She blew out her candle, felt her way to the gate, and crept out into the passage where Miss Moldavia and Lionel had disappeared.

The Ashby dungeons were not very large. In the old days hardly anyone had been held there, and since the Invasion a new, huge jail had been built on the outskirts of town. The dungeons were badly lit and smelled of damp, but fortunately they were empty. So when Lily heard a voice coming from a room at the end of the single long corridor, she knew it must be Miss Moldavia's.

Wishing more than ever she had Queen Dragon's cape of invisibility, she crept up to the door and peered through the grille. Sure enough, Miss Moldavia was inside, pacing up and down, while Lionel, the librarian—Prince Alwyn of Ashby—sat tied to a chair and shook his head. Lily overheard a snatch of the conversation.

"You can do what you like to me," said Lionel. "Kill me, drop me into the moat. I'll never marry you, and I'll never be king while there's a single Black Squad left in Ashby."

"Enough!" snarled Miss Moldavia. "Have you forgotten I have Evangeline Bright down at the grommet factory? Think of her, shoveling coal into the blast furnace. I can have her up here in this room in half an hour, undergoing the most exquisite tortures before your very eyes...The rack. The thumbscrews. The iron maiden. It's a fine thing to be brave yourself, but let's see what you think when it's someone else's pain you're watching."

"You wouldn't dare—" Lionel cried, and he struggled wildly in his chair. But Lily did not hear the rest of his reply. For as she strained on tiptoes to see, a strong hand in a black leather glove came down heavily on her shoulder, spun her around, and slammed her back against the door of the cell.

"Well, well, well," said a familiar voice. "If it isn't Lily Quench."

It was Captain Zouche.

# chapter eleven
# Prince Alwyn

"Molly!" yelled Captain Zouche. "Molly? Are you in there?"

His grip tightened cruelly on Lily's shoulder as she struggled and kicked his shins.

"Let me go! Let me go!" Suddenly, the studded door of the interrogation room creaked open. Lily fell backward into the room. She grabbed at something as she fell, realized it was Miss Moldavia's leg, and landed in a heap at her feet.

"Ouch!"

Miss Moldavia shook off Lily's hand and kicked

her aside. Lily yelped and rolled across the floor. She looked up and saw Lionel—Prince Alwyn— tied to a chair. Beside him waited Mr. Trench, the torturer.

"About time we did something about that creep, Molly," said Captain Zouche, eyeing Lionel. "Have you learned anything?"

"Not yet." Miss Moldavia looked at Lily, who was cowering on the floor. "Well, well. If it isn't Lily Quench. Where did you find her, Zouchey?"

"She was lurking outside," said the captain. "I was coming to tell you that the dragon's been sighted again, in Ashby Thicket. I found Miss Quench listening at the door."

"I suppose she came with the dragon," said Miss Moldavia. "Never mind. I'll soon deal with it. As a matter of fact, Zouchey, I'd already heard about the dragon. A Black Squad is on the way, armed with poisonous blow darts. Monkey Island has supplied us with the recipe, and I've ordered a triple dose." She smiled. "That should provide a permanent solution to my first problem. And Lily Quench is the solution to the second."

Captain Zouche looked blank. "The second?"

"The missing prince, Zouchey," said Miss

Moldavia. "I can't believe you've already forgotten I was trying to find him. In the end, it wasn't very hard. May I introduce my fiancé, Prince—or should I say, King—Alwyn Lionel of Ashby?"

"That creep?" Captain Zouche was aghast. "Molly, I thought you would have had more taste."

"I admit he's not really my type," Miss Moldavia agreed. "But he is king of Ashby, and since I intend to be queen he will have to do. In fact, now I have Lily Quench we can hold the coronation right after the wedding. What a pity you won't be able to attend."

"Hang on a moment," said Captain Zouche. The wheels in his head ground slowly, but they were grinding all the same. "You can't be queen, Molly. The Black Count rules Ashby. And I'm in charge for him."

"Not anymore, you're not," said Miss Moldavia, and as she spoke Lily became aware of the sound of footsteps echoing hollowly in the dungeon corridor. "Ah. There's the squad come to take you to the grommet factory. Good-bye, Captain Zouche. I wish I could say it's been a pleasure working for you, but it hasn't. My only consolation will be that when I am queen I won't have to listen to you SCREAMING ANYMORE!"

Queen Dragon lay nestled in the leaf litter in the forest clearing, waiting for the sun to rise above the trees. She was tired, hungry, and worried about Lily. Though Lily did not know it, Queen Dragon had a very high opinion of her abilities. But she also knew Lily was still young in the ways of Quenching, and that there was always a chance something might go unexpectedly wrong with their plan.

Like now...

Branches rustled quietly in the undergrowth, and a faint scent of human being floated toward her. Queen Dragon's half-closed eyes snapped open. Someone was creeping through the forest. Had she and Lily been seen? Fire rumbled in Queen Dragon's throat, and she let a warning trickle of smoke float from her nostrils. The rustling noises paused for a moment, then the bushes parted to reveal a weedy little boy.

Queen Dragon felt a rush of relief. Harmless.

At least, she was pretty sure he was, unless he had bigger friends following. Oddly enough, he did not seem at all frightened by her, but merely stood staring at her as if he had never seen anything so marvelous in all his life. Which, Queen Dragon reflected, he probably hadn't.

"Well, boy? What do you want?" Queen Dragon said. "Didn't your mother teach you it was rude to stare?"

"You can talk!" said the boy, and then, as if he had finally remembered his manners, he bowed deeply. "Jason Pearl, ma'am, at your service."

"And I'm Sinhault Fierdaze. Queen Dragon to my human friends. You haven't answered my question, Jason Pearl. What do you want? Or are you just here to stare?"

Jason shook his head. "I've come to help you, Queen Dragon. My father is the keeper of Ashby Thicket; he works for Miss Moldavia. You see, she has my mother working in the grommet factory. When Father saw you land earlier this evening, he went straight to the castle to tell her. By now a Black Squad will probably already be on its way."

"A Black Squad?" Queen Dragon sat up. Smoke poured from her mouth and nostrils in dismay. Jason

coughed and flapped his hand in front of his face.
"That's right," he said. "If I were you, I'd
skedaddle. Vamoose. Right now."

"But I can't," wailed Queen Dragon. "There's
Lily, and Prince Alwyn and the plan—oh, it's all
too complicated! Everything's gone wrong! What
on earth am I going to do?"

"Prince Alwyn!" Jason exclaimed. "Do you
mean he's alive?"

"He's in Ashby Castle," said Queen Dragon.
"My friend Lily Quench has gone there to crown
him, and now you're telling me Miss Moldavia
knows we're here. Which means Lily has walked
into a trap!"

As she spoke, Queen Dragon heard faint voices
coming from the edge of the thicket. Feet
marched along the road, and an engine roared.
Queen Dragon looked at Jason, and he looked
back at her. Their eyes were wide with fear.

"Army boots," said Jason. "It's the Black Squad.
And a truck."

Queen Dragon shook her head. "No," she said.
"I know that sound. It's not a truck. It's a tank.
I think we'd better—"

"Vamoose," said Jason as he jumped up onto

her nose. "You know, I've always wondered what it's like to fly."

A few moments later the Black Squad, beating its way through the thicket, was surprised by the scent of smoke and the sound of branches crashing and splintering. Streaming fire and sparks, a huge black object shot like a cannonball out of the trees. Only one soldier kept his head long enough to fire off a bazooka full of sleep darts, but by then it was too late. The dragon was already headed in the direction of Ashby Water, the castle, and Miss Moldavia.

The sound of his cell gate opening brought Mr. Hartley out of unconsciousness. He was so exhausted, and in such pain from being chained to the wall of the dungeon, that he had passed out soon after Lily left him. Footsteps sounded on the stone floor of the cell and a hand grabbed his wrist and unlocked his manacles. Mr. Hartley groaned as the chains fell from his wrists, tried to sit up, but fell heavily on the floor instead.

"Get up," said a voice, and Mr. Hartley opened

his eyes. Mr. Trench stood above him, together with two Black Squad soldiers carrying torches. After so long in the dark, the light made Mr. Hartley's eyes ache and water. It was time, then. The rats were waiting. Mr. Hartley tried to feel brave, but after all he had been through, it was hard to keep up his spirits.

But instead of taking him to the torture chamber, the soldiers produced a basin and some soap and water, a razor, and some clean clothes. With rough hands, they washed, shaved, and dressed him. Mr. Hartley let them do it. He was too weak to fight them.

"What's happening?" he murmured as they dragged him toward the entrance of the secret tunnel. "Where are you taking me?"

"To the church, of course," said Mr. Trench, with an unpleasant smile. "Where else would one hold a wedding?"

Lily sat in the vestry of Ashby Church, her hands tied tightly in front of her. Beside her sat Lionel. He was dressed in a very grand uniform Miss

Moldavia had borrowed from Captain Zouche, but since Lionel was tall, his wrists and ankles stuck out awkwardly at the cuffs and made him look even more uncomfortable than he was.

On the vestry table was a huge box, bound with iron bands and locked with a huge padlock shaped like a dragon's head.

"What's in the box?" asked Lily.

"It's the Great Crown of Ashby," answered Lionel. "All the kings and queens of Ashby have been crowned with it, from the days of Elspeth the Magnificent."

"You don't have to go through with this," said Lily. "You can just say no—refuse to marry her. She can't make you."

Lionel shook his head. "I can't," he said miserably. "If it was just me, it wouldn't matter—but she has Evangeline prisoner, too. The best I can do is go through with the wedding and the coronation, and then try and do something about it afterward."

"It'll be too late then," Lily began, but her voice was drowned out by a fanfare of trumpets. The door opened and Mr. Trench appeared with Mr. Hartley, and the guards.

"It's time," he said. One of the men cut Lily and Lionel's bonds and dragged them to their feet; the other picked up the box with the dragon-head lock. Lily and Lionel gave each other one last, helpless glance and marched out between their captors into the church.

The marriage register lay open on a table, and Mr. Hartley stood at the altar rail, looking faint and sick. Lily had never been to a wedding before, so she did not really know what to expect; but the scene was so grim she was sure this wasn't the way it was supposed to be. The inside of the church was in much the same state of ruin as it had been the last time she saw it, though somebody had shoveled up the pigeon droppings and taken the boards off the windows. Huge candelabras were now in place, dripping wax all over the floor, and the pews were filled to overflowing with members of the Black Squads. Furthermore, enormous pictures of Miss Moldavia had mysteriously been hung all over the walls.

"She's been planning this," whispered Lily, and Lionel nodded. Mr. Trench shot them a frown. He and his henchmen marched them over to stand beside Mr. Hartley, and, as if on a prearranged signal, the Black Squads rose to their feet and clicked their boot heels to attention. There was a pause, and a silence, followed by a roar of engines in the street outside.

The trumpeter blew another blast. A searchlight snapped on and flooded the waiting church with light. Lily screwed up her eyes and clapped her hands over her ears to shut out the approaching din; Lionel winced, and Mr. Hartley flung his arm up over his face. The noise grew louder and louder, and the light grew brighter until suddenly, with a screech and a crash of splintering wood, a black sports car came smashing through the doors of the church and squealed to a halt.

Gasoline fumes filled the building. The searchlight dimmed, a spotlight snapped on, and from the wing door on the side of the car, Miss Moldavia emerged.

She was dressed in a long black gown, a jet tiara, and a smoke-colored veil. Her green eyes glinted through the tulle, and her red, painted lips were smiling. Slowly, she climbed out of the car and started walking down the aisle toward her bridegroom. The Black Squads saluted and went down on one knee.

Miss Moldavia reached the altar rail and stretched out a thin black-gloved hand for Lionel's arm. Mr. Hartley looked at Lionel. Lionel nodded faintly, and closed his eyes.

"Welcome. Welcome, er, friends," said Mr. Hartley in a wavering voice. "We are here tonight to, er, celebrate the marriage of Alwyn Lionel Perceval and"— he bent forward to whisper in Miss Moldavia's ear—"and Agrippina Roxana. If anyone here tonight knows of a reason why we should not proceed with this wedding, I charge them to speak forth now."

He paused. Lily started to open her mouth, felt Mr. Trench's hand twist in her collar, and closed it again. Her eyes flicked sideways to the box containing the Great Crown of Ashby. It was sitting on the table with the marriage register, but the dragon-head lock was still firmly attached to the hasp, and there was no sign of any key.

"Get on with it, then," said Miss Moldavia. "I haven't got all night, you know."

Mr. Hartley cleared his throat. But before another word could leave his mouth, a shrill, ghastly cry sounded in the air outside.

A flash of orange fire ripped like a giant blowtorch past the windows, followed by another. Something huge and hot swooped past, lighting up the night sky, and the building rattled and shook. Smoke filled the air. Lily screamed, and the box containing the crown flew off the table and bounced under a pew.

"Stop it!" shouted Miss Moldavia. "Stop it!"

"It's too late!" cried Mr. Hartley with delight. "The wedding's off!"

The Black Squads erupted in pandemonium, and Miss Moldavia disappeared from view. Meanwhile, the church shivered to its foundations as something huge and hideous landed on the roof and started smashing the rafters.

## chapter twelve
# The Battle for Ashby Water

"It's the dragon!" shouted Mr. Trench. He let go of Lily's shoulder. "She's brought the dragon with her!"

Queen Dragon roared once again, and a streak of flame shot through the hole in the roof and licked at the woodwork. Smoke filled the building, and the soldiers milled about. Some of them had run amok and were fighting among themselves; others pulled out their bazookas and blasted useless holes in the church walls.

Lionel was struggling with Miss Moldavia, who

was grabbing him by the arm. A panicking soldier aimed a bazooka straight at them.

"No, fool!" yelled Miss Moldavia, and she and everyone at the front of the church dived for safety as part of the wall exploded in a shower of rubble and plaster dust. Mr. Hartley, Lionel, and the box containing the crown flew into a corner and lay tangled up with the ruined table. Lily flipped head over heels and ended up under a pew. She coughed, and flapped her hand in front of her face, then saw that Miss Moldavia had landed beside her. She was all tied up in her bridal veil, and her glittering dress was covered with dust.

Terrified, Lily started to back away from her. But as Miss Moldavia fought to free herself from the wreckage, Lily saw something that made her forget her mother had ever been a Cornstalk. A small bronze key with a dragon coiled around the shaft was hanging on a chain around Miss Moldavia's neck. Lily had never seen it before, but she recognized it immediately, for the key, like the box containing the crown, was the property of the Quenches. It had hung around the necks of Brian and Matilda, and been stolen from her father as he lay dying on the ramparts of Ashby Castle during the Siege. A great rage came over Lily. She grabbed the key and yanked down on it with all her strength.

Miss Moldavia shrieked and struck out, but Lily held fast. When Miss Moldavia tried to get up, she tugged again so hard Miss Moldavia lost her balance and went toppling forward. Together, they went rolling under the pew, Miss Moldavia's fingernails scratching at Lily's face as she got more and more hopelessly tangled in her veil. Still, Lily would *not* let go of the key. She pulled again, so

hard that the chain bit into Miss Moldavia's neck, and then a weak link suddenly snapped and the key came away in her hand.

Miss Moldavia gave a shout of rage, but Lily

was already wriggling out from under the pew. She ran up the aisle, dodging soldiers and ignoring the screams of Mr. Trench from where he lay, trapped under a pile of rubble. Lionel and Mr. Hartley were in a corner, fighting off a Black Squad soldier with a leg from the broken table. Lily found the box and turned it over. The dragon grinned up at her; she slid the key into its mouth, turned it quickly, and undid the latch.

"Lionel! Quickly!" she shouted above the din, and with one last superhuman effort, Lionel thrust away the soldier and sent him sprawling down the steps. Another came running, but Mr. Hartley picked up the marriage register and hit him with it over the head. Lily threw back the lid of the iron box and thrust her hands into the velvet folds within. Something cool and round and hard met her searching fingers, and she pulled it out, tossing the purple covering onto the floor.

Lionel took one look and dropped automatically to his knees. Mr. Hartley knelt beside him, praying. Lily lifted the crown—it was the heaviest thing she had ever picked up in her life—and held it high over Lionel's head. She opened her mouth, and as the words came into her head from nowhere, she cried out in a great voice:

"As a Quench of the line of Brian and Matilda, I crown you, Alwyn Lionel, King of Ashby and all its territories, Lord of Ashby Castle, Dragonfriend." From the roof above came Queen Dragon's roar of approval, and then suddenly the crown was on Lionel's head and he was standing up, a resolute expression on his face.

"Right," he said. "Now, let's get them."

But the Black Squads were already pouring out of the church into the street outside.

"What's happening?" asked Lily. "Where are they going?"

"And where's Miss Moldavia?" said Mr. Hartley. For Miss Moldavia had completely vanished, though whether into the crowd, or into some hiding place in the church, no one could say. Outside, Queen Dragon gave a loud cry and took to the air again. Lily and her friends looked at one another, then ran for the door.

It was still night, but it seemed much darker

than normal. Every Black Squad in Ashby seemed to be milling about in the churchyard and the street outside, and there were even a few tanks driving up and down, their engines grinding, their searchlights swooping over the buildings. When she sniffed the air, Lily realized why it was so dark. The orange glow that normally lit up the sky was totally extinguished. Someone had shut the grommet factory down.

In the distance, she heard the sound of marching feet coming up the hill toward them.

The Black Squads fanned out into battle positions. Mr. Hartley, who was taller than either Lionel or Lily, suddenly grabbed them and pulled them back inside.

"Quickly. Upstairs, into the bell tower!"

The Black Squad officers were shouting orders, and the tanks pushed forward through the soldiers and leveled their guns. Lily hesitated a moment, then started hurrying up the rickety wooden staircase after Lionel and Mr. Hartley. A flight of sleepy pigeons flew up around them as they passed. Lily found herself getting dizzy as she ran around and around, and then suddenly about six feet below the roof of the tower, the steps ran out.

Mr. Hartley grabbed a ladder. "Up you go, Lily," he said, and she climbed through a wooden trapdoor and scrambled out onto the roof of the tower. Apart from the grommet factory chimney, the church tower was the tallest building in Ashby and she could see everything that was happening below. Lily leaned over the edge of the parapet, her hair tossed by the breeze. Behind her, Lionel was also emerging from the trapdoor. He straightened the crown he was still wearing on his head, and stood beside her.

"Evangeline!" he yelled, and Lily looked down the cross street in the direction of the factory. An army of grommeteers was marching determinedly up the hill. At their head, dressed in shapeless factory overalls, was a young woman with dark hair.

She looked up, and Lionel waved from the church tower. At the sight of him, the grommeteers burst into cheers and started charging forward up the hill.

"That's my girl!" shouted Lionel.

"No!" cried Lily. "Lionel, stop them! Look! The tanks!"

Though the unarmed grommeteers could not

yet see them, the tanks were moving through the ranks of the Black Squads, their guns swiveling back and forth as if seeking targets. In another moment, the grommeteers would reach the church, and the tanks would be upon them. Lily jumped up and down and waved her arms, screaming for them to turn back, but the grommeteers only cheered louder. Though they could see her and Lionel on top of the tower, they could not see the army that was lying in wait for them around the corner.

Then, out of nowhere, a huge black shadow blotted out the moon that was shyly peeping through a cloud. Lily ducked, saw Queen Dragon swooping overhead, a small boy perched on her head, and heard the screams from below as the grommeteers and Black Squads scattered alike. All was confusion and panic. Again, Queen Dragon and Jason swooped, this time picking up a tank and hurling it into the river. The dragon took out the grommet factory chimney with one gigantic blast of flame, ignited the roof, and left the building blazing.

"Yes!" screamed Lily ecstatically. "Show them, Queen Dragon, show them!" And leaving Lionel and Mr. Hartley to watch from the parapet, she turned and ran down the ladder so she could join in the fray.

All this time, Miss Moldavia had been hiding in the back of the church. After Lily had seized the key from her, she had waited under a pew until the building was empty, then crept out into the vestry so she could watch through the window. At first, she had thought the battle was going her way. Then she heard the cheers of the grommeteers, saw the fire as Queen Dragon attacked, and realized everything was lost.

Miss Moldavia picked up her skirts and crept back out into the church just as Lily reappeared at the foot of the bell tower. She ducked back hastily into the shadows. Lily did not see her, and in another moment she had passed outside into the night. From the shrieks and thuds that were coming from the street, Miss Moldavia guessed that a furious battle was going on between the remaining Black Squad soldiers and the grommeteers. It was a battle she had no intention of joining.

Miss Moldavia tiptoed over to the sports car she had parked in the entrance of the church. It was Evangeline's, which she had stolen from the parking lot at the castle, but that did not concern her. She wrenched open the driver's door, jumped in, and threw the car into reverse.

With a squeal of rubber, the car shot backward out of the church and into the churchyard. Black Squad soldiers and grommeteers scattered willy-nilly as she swerved through them, changed direction, and headed for the street. A single grommeteer leapt out of the crowd and rushed to close the churchyard gates.

"Stop!" she cried, but Miss Moldavia was already accelerating toward her. For a second, the grommeteer struggled with the bolts on the gate, and then the car screeched past her, catching her side and flinging her to the ground. There was a shower of sparks as the churchyard gates burst open and Miss Moldavia took off down the street and headed for the open road.

Evangeline had always driven her car with the precision of a racing champion. Miss Moldavia was not so skilled, but since she didn't mind denting a few panels along the way, she was still out of Ashby Water and on the open road in under three minutes. The car was fast and hugged the curves; ahead of her, in the light of her one unbroken headlamp, she could just see the dark bulk of Ashby Thicket straddling the road.

Once through the forest, she would take the inland highway and head for the Black Citadel. The Black Count would be appalled to hear of the revolution in Ashby and would send an army to deal with it immediately. The thought of revenge on Lily Quench made Miss Moldavia smile, and she flattened her foot on the car's accelerator.

The noise of the car's engine blocked out most of the outside noise. Not that this would have made any difference, for a dragon's flight can be almost soundless. Miss Moldavia was not aware that Queen Dragon had been following until the very moment she swooped down on her. And by then, it was too late. One crunch. The car was gone.

And so was Miss Moldavia.

Back in Ashby Water, the last of the Black Squads

had surrendered or been driven off. The city belonged to the grommeteers. But around the gate of the churchyard, a little group of people huddled around a still figure in a bloodstained factory uniform.

It was Evangeline.

"I can't feel her pulse," said Mr. Hartley in an anxious voice. "Lily. Have you found any broken bones?"

"Not yet." Lily smoothed the hair back from Evangeline's face and wiped away some blood with her handkerchief. There was an ugly gash on her forehead and scratches across one cheek where she had fallen. Mr. Hartley had already tied a tourniquet around one leg to stop it from bleeding.

Suddenly the crowd parted and Lionel appeared. Everyone went quiet as he knelt beside Evangeline, laid his crown on the ground beside her head, and bent down to listen to her heart.

"It's still beating," he said, and taking her hand in his, he whispered in her ear so softly only Lily and Mr. Hartley could hear.

"Can you hear me, Evangeline? You can't die now. There are so many books for us to read, so many things for us to do. If you die, it will be like getting to the end of the book and finding the final chapter has been torn out. Please wake up, Evangeline. Please. Wake up."

As he finished speaking, Lionel lifted Evangeline's hand to his lips and kissed it. Lily felt a tear trickle down her cheek. She wiped it away, but another swiftly followed it and fell—*plop!*—on Evangeline's face. And at that moment, something incredible happened. Evangeline, who until that moment had been lying as still as death, flinched at the teardrop and fluttered her eyelids.

"She's alive!" shouted Lily. "She's all right!" And as Evangeline's eyes opened hazily, the watching crowd burst into cheers of delight.

"Hmm," said Mr. Hartley. "Looks as if there might be a wedding after all."

## chapter thirteen
# By Quenching We Rule

The celebrations in Ashby went on for days. People danced in the streets, held parties in their homes, hung banners from their windows. Jason Pearl and Mr. Hartley were made knights of the Order of the Boa Spear at a lavish ceremony, while Evangeline, Lily, and Queen Dragon were all made duchesses. King Lionel opened the treasury and found years' worth of money earned from the grommet factory. After setting some aside for working capital, he divided the rest among the grommeteers.

"Now that the factory is gone, they'll need something to set themselves up with," he said to Lily. "And the grommeteers were the ones who earned it, after all. I'm hoping some of them will choose to work in the new gardens." For King Lionel's first decree had been that the grommet factory should be demolished and its site turned back into the Botanic Gardens for the people of Ashby to enjoy.

"My mother would have been very glad of this," said Lily, looking at the plans. "She used to be a gardener, before the Invasion."

"Then we will call them the Liza Cornstalk Memorial Gardens," said King Lionel. "After all your help, Lily, I really think that's the least we can do."

All this time, plans were going ahead for a royal wedding. Evangeline was slowly recovering in Ashby Castle, where it was discovered that, although she was weakened by her accident, her injuries were not as bad as they first seemed. The doctors assured her and Lionel that by the time the marriage took place, she would have fully recovered.

Which indeed, she did.

The marriage of King Lionel and Duchess Evangeline was not the grandest royal celebration ever held in Ashby Water, but it was certainly one of the happiest. Mr. Hartley officiated in the grounds of Ashby Church (the building was in too much of a ruin to be used yet), the bride and bridegroom wore white and silver, and the chief bridesmaid, in primrose satin, was Lily Quench. The best man, somewhat surprisingly, was Wilibald Zouche. For after a stern talking to by Mr. Hartley, the former Captain Zouche had quite reformed.

"Miss Moldavia never knew it," said Mr. Hartley as everyone feasted on the wedding breakfast in the courtyard of Ashby Castle, "but when she sent Zouche to the grommet factory, she did him a favor. You see, as soon as he realized what it was really like to work there, a little chink opened up inside his heart. I think you'll find he'll turn out quite well."

"Which is more than can be said for Miss Moldavia," said Queen Dragon, crunching down on the last of the Black Count's tanks. "That woman gave me the most appalling indigestion I've ever had."

"Miss Moldavia would have been a harder proposition," agreed Mr. Hartley, "but all the same, it could have been done. Unfortunately, I never got the chance to speak to her." He sounded disappointed. Lily, who had other things on her mind, excused herself for a moment and went up onto the highest turret for some fresh air.

It had been a wonderful day, and everything had gone off well. Already, thought Lily as she leaned over the battlements, Ashby Water was a very different place from the town she had grown up in. But somehow, because it was different, she no longer fitted in. And as she watched the twinkling lights of the bonfires lit across Ashby in honor of the occasion, she thought of a conversation she'd had that morning with Evangeline and Lionel and another she'd had with Queen Dragon, and she wondered what she ought to do.

The kings and queens of Ashby had always had a Quench as their adviser. Lily's grandmother Ursula and her father, Godfrey, had both worked for old King Alwyn. It was written in the royal motto: By Quenching We Rule. If that was true, her duty was to stay with Evangeline and Lionel as their official Quencher. But Lily was not sure that was what she wanted to do.

"Have you thought about my proposal?" said a voice. Lily turned and saw King Lionel standing behind her. He was still dressed in his wedding finery with his crown on his head. Despite this, he looked tired and rather careworn.

"Yes," she began, and stopped. Lionel waited for her to go on. When she didn't, he came over to the battlements and stood beside her. The wind whipped through his curly hair, and he looked sad.

"It's not what you want, is it?" he said. "Well, I can understand that. I'm pleased things here are changing and I'm very glad Miss Moldavia's gone, but I've already realized that being a librarian was much more fun than being a king. But I guess I have no choice in the matter. Being a king is what I was born to do."

Lily's heart sank within her. "You mean, like being a Quench?"

"Sort of," said Lionel, "but not exactly. You see, Lily, I've been thinking about this a lot. You're not just a Quench, you're a Cornstalk as well. Quenches love adventure; they like to be in the thick of things. But Cornstalks don't. So tell me. If I were to ask you, as a Cornstalk, what you'd like to do, what would your answer be?"

A picture of Skansey, the Island of Apples, with its ruined huts and orchard, came into Lily's head. She saw a garden with daffodils and lilies and a small, green house with a red roof, and a landing place on the foreshore for a dragon. And she saw herself, sitting on Queen Dragon's head and flying off in search of adventures. For although Lily was a Cornstalk, she was also a Quench. Tonight, for the first time, she had finally realized that the two could not be separated.

"Your Majesty," she said slowly, "I've been thinking a lot about this. I've come to realize that being a Quench has nothing to do with wanting to kill dragons. It's to do with wanting to quench anything that's bad, or ugly, or that spoils people's lives. But the funny thing is, being a Cornstalk's the same. Cornstalks love peace and quiet and beautiful things; they love to make things grow. They're after the same things as a Quench, only they go about getting them in a different way. And to do that, they need time and space to themselves.

"So yes, I would like to be your official Quencher—as long as I can be your official Cornstalk as well."

"Agreed," said King Lionel, and he and Lily smiled and shook hands on their bargain. Together they returned to the courtyard where the guests and Queen Evangeline were waiting.

The wedding cake was cut, and toasts were drunk to Lily, Queen Dragon, and all the friends of the king and queen. Then the chamberlain, Sir Jason Pearl, announced the royal fireworks and everyone went up onto the battlements. Lily, who had been waiting for a chance to creep away, politely took leave of her hosts and went outside to where Queen Dragon was waiting.

"Did you sort it out?" asked Queen Dragon. "No. No need to tell me. I can see from your face that you have."

"Let's go," said Lily.

The first flight of rockets exploded overhead in a shower of red and silver as Lily climbed onto her usual place on Queen Dragon's head. The dragon spread her mighty wings and sprang into the air. She and Lily swooped over the Ashby grommet factory, the river, and the church with the broken door. They sailed over the castle and sent the weathervane on the town hall spinning. Then, with a triumphant spurt of fire from Queen Dragon's nostrils, they left Ashby Water behind them and quickly disappeared among the circling stars.